Grayson North
Frost-Keeper
of the Windy City

by
Kevin M. Folliard

From
Dark Owl Publishing, LLC

Arizona

Cover image by James T Molloy
https://jamestmolloy.storenvy.com
On Instagram @jamestmolloy

Cover design by Dark Owl Publishing

Snowflake image by kropekk pl from Pixabay

Visit us on our website at:
www.darkowlpublishing.com

More YR Novels from Dark Owl Publishing

Dragons of the Ashfall
Book One of the War of Leaves and Scales
An epic steampunk fantasy story
by Jonathon Mast

In addition, all books from Dark Owl Publishing are appropriate for at least teenagers to read.

Please see the Young Readers Bookstore page
on our website
for details on age appropriateness.

www.darkowlpublishing.com/the-yr-bookstore

*For my brother and all the first responders
who keep us safe.*

Chapter 1

"**E**xcuse me! Coming through! Pardon me!" Grayson North sprinted toward the Red Line train entrance. The rising summer sun blazed, eclipsed just behind a row of Chicago skyscrapers.

"Late kid coming through!"

He dodged around a smiling old woman and leapt toward the underground steps. "Gracious! Be careful!" the woman shouted.

Grayson hopped onto the bannister and slid. "It's all right, ma'am!" Cool air chilled his sweat-soaked t-shirt as he descended into the air conditioned station. "I've done this at least ten times!"

He landed feet first onto concrete.

"Whoa-ho! Easy there, daredevil!" a security guard shouted.

"It's okay!" Grayson dashed toward the turnstile. "I've been late before. I know what I'm doing!" Grayson flicked his transit card from his cargo shorts and tapped it to the touchscreen. A bright green *GO* flashed, and he pushed through the bars.

He hurried down the next set of stairs to the humming *click-clack* of the Chicago El Train.

"Please, please! Please be arriving and not leaving!" He jumped past the final five steps and raced across the platform.

The loudspeakers chimed. *"Caution! Doors closing!"*

"No!" Grayson slapped the metal door as the train pulled away. "Argh!"

The silver cars disappeared down the dark underground tunnel. Grayson's heart pulsed with exhaustion. He collapsed on a bench to catch his breath.

"What's the hurry?" A trim, white-haired man in suit pants and a gray vest loomed over him. "There's always another train."

"Not one that gets me to work on time. My brother is going to kill me!"

The man sat. "I doubt that."

Grayson sighed. "He's my manager, and he threatened to literally strangle me if I'm late again."

"Aren't you a little young for a summer job?"

"I'm thirteen. I can work up to twenty hours a week." Grayson glanced at the monitor. The next scheduled train would arrive in five minutes.

The man studied Grayson. "What kind of work do you do?"

"I scoop ice cream." Grayson eyed the man suspiciously. "Did you think I would be an accountant?"

"You've got spunk, kid." He rubbed his chin. "I'm not surprised."

A group of teenaged girls giggled and fanned themselves as they bounced down the steps.

"No offense, dude, but you're weirding me out." Grayson stood. "I'm going to wait over there. Have a good one."

"Certainly."

Grayson headed toward the giddy pack of girls. He paused beside the reflective glass surface of a Chicago theater advertisement to check his looks. He wiped the sweat off his forehead with the top of his t-shirt and swept his thick dark hair to one side.

Maybe these girls will hang out with me on the train, he hoped. *Maybe they'll visit me for ice cream.*

The girls fast-talked about so-and-so's boyfriend, that cute top, hanging out at the beach, and of course, the brutal July heatwave. Grayson guessed they were around sixteen. He strutted forward.

"Hey!" he said.

They continued to chatter amongst themselves.

"Hey!" Grayson said louder.

The blonde smiled at him. "Oh hi, little boy. Are you lost?"

"I—little? No." Grayson flushed. He spoke lower, "That guy over there was acting weird, and—"

"Do you need a babysitter, because Tiffany is very affordable," the brunette declared.

"Amber!" her friend shouted. "That's mean!"

"No, seriously. That guy was asking—" Thundering *click-clack* interrupted. The next train slid to a stop and the doors hissed open. The girls tittered their way through the open doors.

The loudspeaker chimed. *"Doors closing!"*

Grayson slipped inside and slunk to a corner seat. The girls chattered at the other end of the car.

The train window reflected Grayson's dejected face. He had the same smooth complexion and blend of Asian and Germanic features as his older brother Jason—except for his unnaturally ice-blue irises.

His eye-color contrasted with his Chinese eyes and thick dark hair. His parents always told him it made him uniquely handsome. Grayson thought his eyes made him look odd. The ugly mole that dotted his chin didn't help either.

Grayson hoped that one day he would fill out like his eighteen-year-old brother: tall, muscular, perfect skin. But even if he had Jason's build and complexion, he'd never have his charm or *Maxim Magazine* face. Jason had a way of approaching girls that mystified and bewildered Grayson. His brother could smile, say a few choice words, and have them hanging off his biceps within minutes.

Grayson was the middle child, stuck between accomplished ladies-man Jason and their genius eleven-year-old brother Mason. Lately, it was getting hard for Grayson to get anyone to notice him. It didn't help that their parents were going through a rocky patch.

Their mom said they were getting divorced.

Jason didn't seem to care. In a few months, he'd be starting college.

Mason never wanted to talk about it. He just buried himself in science fiction books.

Meanwhile, Grayson and his brothers were staying with their mother's sister Linda in Chicago for the summer while their parents sorted things out back in Springfield.

Aunt Linda was one of Grayson's biggest heroes. When Grayson was little, she had gone to culinary school part time and managed restaurants. Growing up, Grayson and his family would visit her at the different places she worked: diners, sushi houses, Thai places, Italian bistros, French pastry shops, and more.

Finally, two years ago, Aunt Linda became a contestant on the prime time reality show *The*

Chopping Block, where she went head-to-head with America's up and coming culinary elite.

She won. After the show, Aunt Linda finally got her big break as a Cuisine Channel celebrity. Now she was opening her own restaurant and ice cream shop at the swanky new Slynt Hotel on the Chicago River, in the heart of downtown.

Jason managed day shifts at Something Suite, the hotel's ice cream shop, while Grayson worked part time a few days a week. Or at least, he *had* been employed there. He glanced at his phone. His shift had started two minutes ago. Maybe he was fired.

"The next stop will be Lake," came the recorded voice. *"Doors open on the left, at Lake."*

Grayson made his way toward the door. To his right, the teenaged girls continued to chatter, but something to his left caught his eye. In the next car over, through the window, the man with the white hair and gray vest also waited by the door. And stared at him.

Hairs bristled on Grayson's neck. He had thought the guy was odd, but now he was thinking he should make a beeline for the nearest cop.

"This is Lake." The train glided to a stop. The doors slid open, and Grayson hurried across the platform. The Red Line tunnel connected underground to the Slynt Hotel lobby. Grayson maneuvered around passing commuters. "Pardon me! Sorry! Late for work!"

He pushed through the turnstile. His footfalls echoed down the white brick tunnel.

Something grabbed his arm. Grayson shouted and screamed.

The man with the white hair held him. "Please! Young man! Quiet!" His voice came out a harsh whisper.

Grayson shouted louder.

"I'm *not* here to hurt you! I promise!"

Grayson wrenched free and tried to run, but the man snatched him from behind and covered his mouth. "Please! I am *so* sorry to frighten you, but time is not on our side."

Grayson bit the man's finger hard.

"Ow!" He uncovered Grayson's mouth. "You don't understand. You're being chased!"

"Yeah!" Grayson shouted. "By you!"

"No! By *them*!" The man placed a narrow metal object between Grayson's hands. "Take this and go! Keep it safe, always!" The man released him and took a step back.

A strange calm washed over Grayson. An icy chill prickled his fingers, cooled his wrist. It was an entirely new sensation, like blasts of air conditioning, rushing through his arm.

"You feel it, don't you?" The man whispered. "Courage coursing through your blood. The gut instinct of centuries of Frost-Keepers."

Grayson's heartbeat steadied. A calming cold swelled inside his chest.

The man pointed to Grayson's hands. "The Frost-Key—the Frost-*Blade*—is yours now."

"Blade?" Grayson unfolded his fingers to reveal a silvery key with shimmering copper bands. The metal was icy to the touch. Chills washed over his shoulders, cooled his face.

He finally noticed the man's unnaturally ice-blue eyes, so much like his own.

The man placed his hand on Grayson's shoulder. "I am sorry our time is brief. Victor will explain more. For now, take this key, and run!"

Grayson puzzled over the silvery key, freezing his palms like an ice cube. But the cold caused no pain or discomfort. Cool vapor streamed from Grayson's lips onto his hands. "Who's Victor?"

"My ancestor. He was—"

A loud, *prick-prock* sound echoed down the tunnel. The stranger's blue eyes widened. "Hide!" He pointed at a vending machine and trash can. "Now!"

Grayson clutched the ice-cold key and scrambled toward the vending machine. He wedged himself behind the plastic garbage can and peeked out. The *prick-prock* grew louder. Closer.

"You outmaneuvered me at O'Hare, envoy," came a snide, female voice. "But your heat signature was easy to track, even in this glorious weather."

The man raised his arms in surrender and slowly turned to face his pursuer.

A tall, curvaceous woman strutted into view. Her red platform heels echoed against the concrete. She tossed back waves of fiery red hair.

"Scarlett Fury," the stranger said. "Your reputation for horrors precedes you."

"Flattery will get you nowhere, old man." The woman wore sunglasses and bright red lipstick. A crimson dress hugged her attractive hourglass shape. "You cannot run. Place the Frost-Key on the ground in front of you."

"I never had the key." The man shrugged. "My job was to lead you away from the true envoy."

"Liar!" The woman removed her black sunglasses. Her eyes glowed yellow.

Grayson's heart hammered. The icy key cooled his hands. His body froze still as a statue.

"I do not fear you, Sulfurian," the man said. "Do your worst. I've done my part."

"Enjoy your last precious seconds as you savor such a small, pitiful victory, human." The woman laughed. "Soon this oblivious city will once again know our rage. And like you, they will all burn."

The woman's mouth widened into a circular O-shape. The round cavity expanded like a rubber band until it took up her whole face. The skin of her head peeled into accordion folds, down her neck and past her shoulders.

A hideous creature glowed and twitched out from beneath the folds of skin that had been the woman's head and torso. A spherical face snarled. Eyes blistered. Her skin was charred like blackened meat. White-hot talons flexed at the ends of her bony arms. The creature resembled a giant living matchstick.

She glowed brighter and brighter, until blinding yellow light cooked the tunnel.

Grayson clutched his key and squeezed his eyes shut. A protective, icy cocoon enveloped his body.

The intense light subsided. Spots danced over Grayson's vision as the matchstick creature twisted and gave a smoke-filled laugh.

Black soot streaked the concrete where the white-haired man had stood.

Chapter 2

The creature's skin folded over her shoulders and up her neck. She fixed her human face and hair into place and tossed her red locks.

Grayson crouched low. Held his breath.

The woman placed her sunglasses over her glowing yellow eyes, then she glanced back and forth down the empty tunnel. She traced her fingers in a wide circle and carved an oval of fire in midair.

An orange face, with a beard of flames, radiated in the center of the oval.

"Where is the Frost-Key?" the voice rumbled like a volcano.

"I caught the envoy going down a commuter tunnel. We flanked the tunnel with mages to repel witnesses." The woman groaned. "But he was a decoy. He knew we would return to Chicago to spawn. The true envoy must be close. I will find the key."

"No!" the fiery face echoed.

The woman scowled. "No?"

"You failed. By now, the key has been passed on. By the time you locate the new Frost-Keeper, it will no

longer be a key. To even touch the blade will doom any Sulfurian. Even you, Scarlett Fury."

The woman gave a scornful laugh. "I fear nothing!"

"*You were bred to be our best warrior, but you have never faced the likes of this enemy,*" the face boomed. "*Our primary mission is to spawn. Let the Frost-Keeper come to us if he dares.*"

"The Frost-Key will be passed on to a novice. A child!" Scarlett Fury snickered. "Impulsive. Weak."

Grayson trembled. His breath steamed.

The face gave a smoky laugh. "*Do not underestimate the collective experience of the Frost-Keepers. He will show himself soon. For now, focus on the host. The Sulfurian legacy takes priority.*"

"As you wish, Great Leader!" The woman flicked her wrists and the fiery portal dissipated into smoke. Her heels *prick-procked* as she stalked back toward the train platform.

Grayson remained still. He gripped the silvery key until her footfalls faded. Then he raced in the opposite direction. The tunnel branched between the Riverwalk and the hotel lobby. A group of commuters turned and stared as he rushed by.

In his haste, Grayson stumbled and tripped. He skinned his knee on the concrete floor. Grayson grimaced as he sat back up. He prepared to take off again, when a firm grip clenched his shoulder.

"Stay back!" Grayson wrenched away, fully expecting the fiery eyes of the red-headed woman.

"Easy, kid!" A dark-haired, uniformed police officer—with normal human eyes—towered over him. "What's the hurry?" The officer helped Grayson to his feet.

"I don't... I..." Grayson struggled to catch his breath.

"Everything okay?"

Grayson shuddered. "Um... not really."

The officer put his hands on Grayson's shoulders. "I'm Officer Lucas. What's your name?"

"Grayson," he panted. "Grayson North."

"Are you in trouble, Grayson?" His eyes narrowed. "You're white as a sheet."

"I... there was this guy. And then this lady was on fire, and she just..." Grayson's finger shook as he pointed down the tunnel toward where the man had been incinerated. He locked eyes with Officer Lucas. He felt the freezing cold metal of the key still in his hand. "You won't believe me."

"Try me. Just take a deep breath. Go as slow as you need to, okay?"

"Okay." Grayson inhaled. "This guy was following me on the train, so I bolted toward the Slynt Hotel where I work. But he caught up and... Well, it turned out he didn't want to hurt me."

"So, it was a misunderstanding?"

"Yeah, but then this crazy lady—you couldn't miss her—she had a bright red dress and red hair and black shades. She came out of nowhere and scorched the guy right in front of my eyes, right by the vending machine!"

"Scorched him how?"

"She spewed fire right out of her ugly monster face! It was..."

Officer Lucas suppressed a smile.

"It was... crazy."

"Sounds like it. But you're okay, Grayson. Take another deep breath."

Grayson breathed in and out.

"Show me where it happened." The officer guided Grayson back down the commuter tunnel, toward the vending machines. "This is where you saw something weird, huh?"

Grayson tensed up. "Yeah, right on this spot."

"Well, take a look." The officer gestured at the tiles. "I don't see anything."

Grayson examined the floor. There *had* been a mark before, and a smoky smell lingering in the air. But now there was nothing.

"I'm not lying, I swear!" Grayson insisted. "It happened. The guy gave me this key!" Grayson held up the key, then did a double take. He was holding a small silvery flashlight, with copper bands. "What the...?"

The officer took the flashlight and examined it. "This is ice-cold," he observed. He clicked the button and shined a bright white light. "Is this real silver? You say the man gave you this? Or he gave you a key?"

"Uh..." Grayson stuttered. "He gave me this... keep... sake. He gave me a keepsake. It's a flashlight... obviously." Grayson's face flushed with embarrassment. He could have sworn he had been holding a key. The whole incident had been so real.

"Grayson, I can tell you're upset. You're shaking. You're sweating. And I don't think you're lying." Officer Lucas clicked the flashlight off and handed it back to Grayson.

"You don't?"

"Nope. There's a heat index today of 104 degrees. You were in a big hurry to get to work on time, right?"

Grayson nodded.

"I think you were stressed and got overheated. You need to be careful. Drink plenty of water."

"I swear to God, it happened, Officer Lucas," Grayson said. "At least I think it happened."

"How about this," Officer Lucas said. "I'll walk you up to the hotel lobby. I can tell your boss you got delayed and it's not your fault, and on my way back, I will keep my eyes peeled for this lady in the red dress. Sound good?"

Grayson nodded. "Okay. Thanks."

"Not a problem." Officer Lucas pressed the button on his radio. "Hey, Bill. Everything's fine down here. A kid was in a rush and got a little overheated."

The radio crackled: "Another one, huh?"

Officer Lucas clicked the button. "Yep. I'm going to walk him upstairs. I'll meet you outside the Slynt Hotel lobby."

The radio crackled. "Copy that."

Grayson and Officer Lucas headed toward the escalator beneath the hotel. "Hey, Officer Lucas?" Grayson asked. "I get that maybe I got overheated or whatever. But the train ride here was air conditioned."

"Sometimes it sneaks up on you. Stay hydrated."

"Gotcha." Grayson squeezed the silver and copper flashlight. The metal still felt like ice, but his hands weren't freezing.

Chapter 3

The Slynt Hotel had been open less than a year. The lobby featured sleek modern furniture, stark industrial light fixtures, and a white marble front desk with the name SLYNT stylishly backlit by soft blue lights. Officer Lucas escorted Grayson past the huge, circular emblem of the Slynt family crest that led to the brass doors of the main elevators.

Hotel tycoon and billionaire industrialist Alexander Slynt had personally chosen Grayson's Aunt Linda as the featured restauranteur of the hotel. It was the biggest break of her career, and she'd moved to downtown Chicago to personally oversee the restaurant and dessert shop.

The restaurant, Linda Liu's Sushi & Steakhouse, was located in the lobby, connected by a joint kitchen to Linda Liu's Something Suite, managed by Grayson's older brother, Jason. The ice cream shop had white marble counters and chrome freezer cases, with neon pink lights that swirled like strawberry syrup.

Grayson's six-foot-one, muscular brother manned the cash register. He wore a form-fitting pink Linda

Liu's Something Suite t-shirt that, despite being pink, somehow managed to make him look even manlier. He charmed two well-dressed older ladies as he handed them twin scoops of French vanilla on sugar cones, wrapped in brown napkins. "Enjoy your stay at the Slynt. I hope you'll come back and visit us again!"

The ladies giggled. "Of course we will! Thank you so much!" The woman dropped a five dollar bill in the tip jar.

As the customers exited the side doors to the Riverwalk, Jason's customer-service smile faded beneath dagger eyes—a glare reserved exclusively for his brother. "You are really late!" His face sagged as he noticed Officer Lucas. "What did he do this time?"

"Nothing," Officer Lucas said. "Your brother got a little overheated on his way here, that's all. I made him stop and rest. It's not his fault."

Grayson folded his arms in satisfaction.

Jason rolled his eyes. "Oh. Well... thanks, I guess."

"Hey!" Officer Lucas pointed to a black and white photo of Aunt Linda on the menu sign. "Chef Linda!"

"Are you a *Chopping Block* fan, Officer Lucas?" Grayson asked.

The officer's eyes lit up. "Oh man, the biggest ever! Linda made a prize winning chocolate soufflé out of nothing but baking powder and a candy bar!"

"Yeah, that was a good one." Grayson rubbed his chin. He glanced at Officer Lucas's bare fingers. "You know, our Aunt Linda is single."

"Grayson!" Jason snapped.

Officer Lucas laughed. "Your aunt? No way!"

"Get to work, Cupid." Jason snatched Grayson by the scruff of his shirt and dragged him behind the counter. "Change in back. Grab an apron. I need you to do inventory while it's still slow. The lunch crowd will be here soon."

"All right, all right." Grayson turned back toward the officer, who was still admiring Aunt Linda's menu picture with star-struck eyes. "Thanks, Officer Lucas. Hey, feel free to stop by later. I'll have Aunt Linda sign an autograph. You want any ice cream or anything before you go?"

"No thanks, Grayson. But I will take you up on that autograph. Drink plenty of water, okay?" Officer Lucas saluted and headed back across the lobby.

Back in the kitchen, Grayson changed into his pink Something Suite shirt. He examined himself in the mirror as he strapped an apron over his chest. *How come Jason's pink shirt makes him look cool and mine just looks girly?* he wondered. *It's all those stupid muscles.*

"Grayson!" Jason loomed over him. "I'm telling you right now, I don't care what happened out there, or what you told that cop, but I am sick of you being late. This is the third time, and when you're family, that only makes it more important to be on time—"

"But this guy at the train stop—"

"And you're smart enough not to get dehydrated on a hot day!" Jason softened. He sighed. "Are you okay?"

"I'm fine now." Grayson shrugged. "I just got worked up or something."

"Listen," Jason said. "Aunt Linda did you a huge favor letting you work day shifts this summer—against my advice, need I remind you?"

"You needn't."

"Don't leave your shift mate waiting. It's unprofessional."

"I know that, but—"

"It doesn't seem like you do, because we've already had this conversation."

"Jason, will you just let me say—"

"I know what you're going to say." Jason sighed. "You're just like Dad, Gray. You don't take responsibility when you screw up." He shoved a clipboard and pen against Grayson's chest. "Our little brother could do this job. It's not hard."

Grayson clenched his jaw. He stood as straight as he could. "Listen. Please."

Jason glowered.

"Chew me out every day we work together, all summer, for every stupid thing that goes wrong, whether it's my fault or whether you just *think* it's my fault. I can take it." Grayson's voice changed to a whisper. "But I don't care how many bugs crawl up your butt, or how mad you get. Don't badmouth Dad to me again!"

Grayson shoved past his brother toward the walk-in freezer around the corner.

"You have ten minutes to complete inventory," came Jason's stony voice. "Then I want you out there helping with the line."

Grayson collapsed against the closed freezer door. He slid to the ground, buried his face in his hands, and stifled tears. At the beginning of the summer, when they had found out they'd be staying with Aunt Linda and working for her, Grayson had been so excited. Not just because he thought it would be cool to have a job and make money. He also thought it would be fun to hang out with his older, cooler, smarter brother. He thought they were going to bond, joke around, and escape all the problems their family had been going through. But since day one on the job,

Jason had only gotten nastier.

Jason didn't realize how sorry their dad was. But Grayson knew their dad was working on things, fixing everything while they were away.

Before they left for Chicago, Dad took Grayson and Mason to lunch—Jason had refused. They had milkshakes, burgers, and fries like old times. Dad told corny jokes. He asked them about the last few weeks of school. He took them to the mall and bought them new summer clothes.

When he dropped them off, he let Mason go ahead inside and had a private moment with Grayson in the car. "Gray, buddy, I want you to know something."

For a long minute, Grayson suffered a stony, uncomfortable silence. Then Dad looked away. His lips tightened. Tears trickled down his scruffy face.

It terrified Grayson. His dad had always been a suave guy. Quick with a joke. Level-headed. Strong. Even when their grandparents passed away, Grayson hadn't seen his dad cry.

But as his father collected himself and spoke bluntly, honestly, Grayson started to feel better. "This is not easy for me to say, son. But I screwed up." His voice broke. "I know things don't feel okay now. But I love your mom. I love you boys more than anything."

Grayson cried then, too. His dad hugged him tighter than ever.

"You and your brothers—hey, even your mom—you guys haven't done anything wrong. This isn't on you. It's on *me*. And I'm going to make it all better. I promise you."

All summer long, up until now, Grayson had managed to keep his cool about the situation at home because he knew their dad had a plan. By the time they returned to Springfield, whether his older brother liked it or not, things would go back to normal.

Grayson wiped his eyes on his pink sleeves. He stood and faced the walk-in freezer, then something caught his eye. Above the metal door handle, a silvery rectangle, framed in copper markings, glinted. Grayson had never seen it before.

In the center of the rectangle was a keyhole, spewing cold vapor.

Why is there a keyhole on the freezer all of the sudden? Grayson wondered. For safety purposes, he didn't think the freezer could be locked from outside.

Something chilled Grayson's thigh. He reached into his cargo shorts and felt the icy handle of the flashlight. But when he pulled it out, the object had transformed back into a silvery-copper key. The strange metal of the lock matched the key.

Grayson inserted the key and found it to be a perfect fit. He turned it, and the freezer clicked.

His eyes widened as he opened the huge metal door. Where shelves and stacks of ice cream tubs should have been, a deep tunnel slanted downward. Glistening icicles stabbed from the ceiling. Slick ice coated the walls and floor.

Grayson called to his brother. "Um... Jason?"

No response.

Grayson's breath puffed. Icy air crept up his arms and legs. It felt refreshing. Inviting. He pulled the key from the lock and stepped inside. The door gently shut behind him, plunging him into darkness.

The key in his hand thickened and transformed again. He clicked a button on the handle and a flashlight beam cut across the cavern. The ice cave was impossibly wide. It took up more space than the freezer should have been able to.

Grayson balanced himself and slid down the frozen pathway. He ended up at the bottom of the cavern, against a wall of ice. His flashlight beam caught something hunched by the floor.

Grayson gasped. A frozen man with a snow-crusted beard was trapped, half inside the wall. The man wore a long, frosty coat, leather vest, black gloves and boots, and a thick leather belt, all crystalized in white. His wide-brimmed helmet dripped with icicles.

Snowflakes clung to the man's eyebrows and lashes. His fingertips were pale blue. He looked like he had been dead for centuries.

Grayson inched closer and shined his light against the man's face. The frozen eyes popped open.

Chapter 4

Grayson shouted and slipped backward. A white cloud escaped the man's lips as he unleashed a rattling gasp. Ice cracked and crystals shattered as the man flexed his frozen face.

"Is it time?" his voice grated. "Has it been so long?"

Grayson stared in stunned silence.

The man's arms and legs remained trapped in the ice. His chill blue eyes squinted in the flashlight beam.

"Forgive me," the man said. "But may I see your face? The face of the man who carries our great legacy?"

Grayson trembled to his feet. "I'm sorry, but... I'm not who you think I am. You see, this guy gave me this key, and it turned into a flashlight and—"

"Of course." The man gave a sorrowful laugh. "I forget myself. You are a child. As I was. I am sorry for this burden, but in time you will understand it is a great honor. What is your name, young man?"

"Grayson North. We need to get you out of that ice." Grayson knew the man should be suffering frostbite or hypothermia. "I'm going to get my brother."

"No time!" the man shouted. "And I am in no pain. I merely slept. The ice has kept me safe. It's called cryogenesis."

"Sounds like some kind of retro video game," Grayson said. "But seriously, you look like a human popsicle. That can't be healthy."

"I have seen better days," the man said. "My time is over, Grayson. I'm only here to pass on the power of the Frost-Keeper."

"I keep hearing those words. What exactly is a Frost-Keeper?"

"I *was* the Frost-Keeper." The man smiled. "Now, *you* are." His voice dropped low. "I wish this was a celebratory occasion. But if you have accepted the Frost-Key, it must mean the return of the Sulfurians."

"Sulfurians? That's what that old man called that psychotic matchstick lady!" Grayson took a few steps closer. He shined his light along the man's torso. Beneath blurry ice, he noticed a strange vintage quality to his jacket and vest. "You've been in this ice a long time, haven't you?"

"In cryogenesis, time slipped away quickly for me." Despite being glazed with ice, the man's eyes held profound warmth. "My name is Victor Drake. I am— *was*—the 101st Frost-Keeper to protect the human race. You, Grayson North, are the 102nd. And I know you will honor those who have gone before you."

"Okay, slow down!" Grayson said. "What's a Frost-Keeper? How am I supposed to honor you if I don't even know what I'm supposed to do?"

The man smiled. "The adaptanium weapon you hold would not have chosen you unless you were worthy."

Grayson turned the flashlight over in his hand.

The silvery-copper bands glinted. "It's not a weapon. It's a flashlight. Or a key. It can't seem to make up its mind."

"Adaptanium is a special metal from another world that channels elemental energies. The metal changes form based on need. The Frost-Key is whatever tool of similar size and shape you require, and so much more. When you hold it, the collective instinct of one hundred and one Frost-Keepers cools your blood. The key guided my descendant to you."

"That guy in the subway? I don't know how to say this, but..." Grayson hesitated. *How do I tell him that his descendant is dead?*

"Grayson, I only have so much time, and I want to tell you about your new enemy. The Sulfurians are ruthless, wrathful beings. They will reduce the city to ashes before they give up on their goals. They can hide among humans and manipulate people's minds. Be careful who you trust."

"Who *should* I trust?"

"Do you have a family, Grayson?"

"Yeah," Grayson said. "I have two brothers."

"Trust them. But keep them out of harm's way. Starting today, you are a target. Soon you will know how to fight back, but until you master control of your abilities, I would tell no one about the Frost-Key."

"What abilities?"

Victor wheezed. His voice trembled. "The power transfer is nearly complete."

"Power transfer?"

Victor's skin glazed over. His blue irises turned white as paper. "There are answers... hidden in the tower..."

"What tower?" Grayson reached out. His fingers

slipped off the frozen surface of Victor Drake's shoulder. "Hey, Victor! Stay with me!"

"The tower... was all that remained... I left things for you there... to understand..." Victor's face frosted over. Ice crept toward his lips. "So many lost... but rebirth... inevitable..." Victor's lips froze. Steam swirled from his frozen mouth and faded. Beneath the ice, his human flesh turned crystal clear, like glass.

"Victor? Mr. Drake?" Grayson struggled to shake Victor free, but his frozen form was rock solid. "Please, come back! I need to know what's going on!"

Suddenly, Victor shattered into icy crystals and powdery snow. The frosty residue coated Grayson. He screamed, slipped and fell. He scrambled back up the tunnel, onto his feet. He slipped again and caught himself on the metal freezer door.

Grayson pushed and tumbled back into the warm kitchen storage area. He landed face first on the tiles. "Help! Somebody, help! Please!"

Footsteps echoed and soon Jason's shadow loomed over him. "What the heck is wrong with you?"

Grayson twisted around into a sitting position. "I— the man—the freezer! He exploded!" He pointed into the open freezer.

Metal shelving and stacked towers of cardboard ice cream tubs stared back. The inventory clipboard was face down on the floor.

Jason stepped into the freezer and picked up the clipboard.

"Jason, be careful!" Grayson shouted.

"Man in the freezer?" His brother stepped back out. He examined the clipboard. "What have you been doing all this time? Not inventory." Jason held up the blank sheet and shook his head. "I can't decide if you are pulling the world's lamest practical joke, or if you are *seriously* going insane."

Grayson stood. He cautiously moved behind his brother and stuck his head in the freezer. "No, really. Someone was in here! He was covered in ice. This flashlight! It's some kind of key." Grayson held up his other hand to show his brother.

Jason glowered. "That's not a key *or* a flashlight."

Grayson did a double-take. He was now holding a silvery ice cream scooper. "I... what?" The ice cream scoop had the same coppery bands as the key and flashlight.

"I am really asking, Gray," Jason said. "Are you going insane? Because if so, I can't legally force you to work your shift."

Grayson pushed the enormous freezer door shut. His heart sank. The silver-copper keyhole had disappeared. "What the heck?"

Jason felt Grayson's forehead with the back of his hand. "You feel fine. A little cold, but then again you've been slacking off in the freezer."

"I..." Grayson was about to defend himself, when Victor Drake's words of caution echoed in his mind: *You are a target. Tell no one about the Frost-Key.*

"I... am so sorry, Jace. I meant to do inventory, really." Grayson rubbed his head and shrugged. "Maybe it *is* heat exhaustion. Officer Lucas said it sneaks up on you."

Jason sighed. "Okay. Drink some water. Take five. Screw your head back on." Jason hurried back toward the shopfront. "But if I catch you slacking off even one more time, I'm cutting your hours!"

Grayson reopened the freezer and, once again, saw only stacks of ice cream. Maybe he *was* going crazy.

But a shivery sensation flowed from the handle of

the ice cream scooper. He could feel it, stronger than before. The Frost-Keeper's power flowing into his fingertips.

Grayson squeezed the handle of the ice cream scooper. He had to figure out what was going on. Victor had mentioned a tower, but what tower?

No big deal, he decided. *How many tall buildings can there be in the city of Chicago?*

Chapter 5

By the time Grayson returned to the storefront, Jason was already ringing up a group of customers, laying on his usual charm.

"Can't go wrong with Rocky Road! Single scoop of chocolate on a sugar cone! Hey, little brother! How about a peanut butter and banana shake for this fine fellow over here!"

Above Jason's customer-service-smile, his annoyed glare seemed to say, *Get your act together, Grayson. My pity only goes so far.*

Grayson used the silvery-copper ice cream scooper to dish out one shake order after the next. The line grew longer, and his brother called out order after order. "Banana split! Shortcake sundae! Double scoop of butterscotch ripple in a waffle!"

Grayson hurried from freezer to shake mixer, back to the sundae bar, back to the freezer. He reached for a waffle cone, but his brother snatched it away.

"Too slow!" Jason scooped out the cone, wrapped it in a napkin and handed it to an attractive green-eyed girl across the counter. She giggled and dropped her change in the tip jar. "Thanks, Jason! See you next time!"

They had reached the end of the lunch rush. Once the flirtatious girl was out of earshot, Grayson made a kissy-face. "*Thaaaaanks*, Jason!"

Jason ignored him. "Pick up the pace on those shakes and sundaes, Gray. Time is money in the restaurant business."

"You've been a manager for two months." Grayson rolled his eyes. "Suddenly you're an expert?"

"He's right." Aunt Linda stood with her arms crossed by the open kitchen door. Aunt Linda's straight, black hair was neatly pinned beneath her chef's hat. She wore a pristine white shirt and sleek black pants. Only a powdery hint of flour dusted her hands and cheeks, suggesting she had just assisted the steakhouse prep staff on the other side of the kitchen.

Grayson's short, chunky eleven-year-old brother Mason lurked behind Aunt Linda. He adjusted his thick, black-framed glasses, eyes fixed firmly on the glowing screen of his reading tablet, and absentmindedly scratched his messy black hair.

Mason was smart. Smarter than Jason or Grayson. Except for P.E., he'd never gotten a grade lower than an A-plus. He was also shy. All summer long, Grayson had tried to hang out with his little brother, since Jason was too cool and too busy anyway. But Mason usually preferred the books on his tablet to quality brotherly bonding.

"Here's another wise cliché, Grayson." Aunt Linda pointed to the pink and white splatters on the chrome shake mixer. "Cleanliness is next to godliness."

"Give me a break, Aunt Linda." Grayson huffed over to the shake machine. He removed his latex gloves, grabbed a sanitized towel, and started to scrub away the milky fallout from his last few shakes. "We just beat the rush. Can't I take a breath before I clean?"

"The Slynt Hotel has high standards of excellence," Aunt Linda said. "And I'm meeting Mr. Slynt's entourage right here in five minutes to go over the menu for tonight's engagement party. This place has to sparkle."

Jason wiped the counter and started to prep more cones. "No worries, Aunt Linda. I run a tight ship. Grayson, I want that shake and sundae counter so clean I can see my face in it!"

"How you can see anything with your face so far up your—"

"Grayson!" Aunt Linda surveyed the lobby.

"Gray had a freak-out today," Jason dropped casually.

"I did not!" Grayson snapped.

"A freak-out?" Aunt Linda glanced between the two brothers.

"Heat stroke or something," Jason said. "A *cop* had to escort him to work, and he was late, but I let him off with a warning."

"What?" Aunt Linda's concerned eyes met Grayson's. "Heat stroke is very serious."

"It wasn't heat stroke," Grayson said. "It was more like... heat nudged or something. No big deal. I'm fine. Besides, Officer Lucas is a huge fan. He's coming back for your autograph, Aunt Linda."

"You're okay?" Aunt Linda locked eyes with him.

Grayson nodded.

"Was he cute?"

"I don't want to get your hopes up." Grayson smiled. "But he could be uncle material."

Aunt Linda laughed.

"Grayson freaked out *again* though." Jason sighed dramatically. "In the freezer. Thought he saw a monster or something."

"Turned out it was just a picture of my hideous manager," Grayson said.

"All of my nephews are equally handsome," Aunt Linda said. "Gray, are you sure you're feeling okay?"

"Never better."

"Good. Because when your shift ends, I want you to take Mason to the Chicago History Museum. I promised I'd take him this week, but I'm buried in meetings and prep."

"No problem!" Grayson smiled at his brother. "That's what nephews and brothers are for." He glanced down at the metallic countertop. "And hey look: I *can* see my face!"

"Chef Linda!" A theatrical voice thundered from across the lobby. A well-built middle-aged man with light brown hair and distinguished gray streaks over his ears led an entourage of well-dressed professionals across the lobby. Alexander Slynt wore a pressed black suit and tie, his cash-green eyes gleaming above a wide, enthusiastic smile. A slender but attractive older woman with dark hair and high cheekbones was hooked on his right arm. The woman's eyes were discolored, and Grayson noticed a collapsible blind person's cane tucked beneath her other arm.

In addition to a muscular, dark-skinned security guard in shades, and two aides tapping at their phones, a lean thirty-something blond man in glasses hurried along Mr. Slynt's left side flicking through items on a tablet.

"Mr. Slynt! What a pleasure!" Aunt Linda rounded the counter and greeted Slynt with a warm two-handed shake. "And Joanna! Congratulations on the engagement! I'm so glad we can finally meet and discuss my absolute favorite subject: food!"

Slynt laughed long and hard. "Yours and mine both, Chef Linda!"

The dark-haired woman shook Aunt Linda's hand. She had a vacant look about her as she spoke. "Chef Linda, I am so sorry, but I have a thousand errands to run before the party. Unfortunately, I won't be able to stay for the tasting."

"Well, fortunately, we both know your fiancé has exquisite taste," Aunt Linda said. "I think we can trust him."

Joanna kissed Slynt on the cheek. Then she paused, tilted her head, and seemed to stare directly at Grayson. Grayson gazed into her faded milky eyes. *She's blind.* A chill ran down his spine. *So why do I feel like she's staring right at me?*

The woman's lips curved into a smile. Grayson's breath caught in his chest. Her smile instantly reminded him of Scarlett Fury of the Red Line. Smug. Arrogant. Cruel.

Grayson's skin crawled. His ice cream scooper froze in his fingertips.

The blond man with the tablet touched Joanna's shoulder. "Ms. Crisp, don't forget, we only have a twenty-minute window for our teleconference with the shareholders on the West Coast, after which Mr. Slynt meets you in the lobby for this afternoon's press event. Make sure you meet us in the penthouse at—"

"Three, yes." Joanna broke her pseudo-gaze away from Grayson, and he instantly felt at ease once more. The metal scooper warmed against his fingers.

Joanna unfolded her cane and extended it to the

floor. "I eagerly await our feast, Linda! The evening will be a smashing success!" She took one last furtive glance in Grayson's direction, then headed back across the lobby, swaying the tip of her cane in front of her. A member of Slynt's entourage broke off and joined her.

As Joanna left, Grayson finally noticed a girl about his age, standing toward the back of Slynt's group. The girl glared as Slynt's fiancée disappeared around the corner.

The blond man adjusted his glasses, scanned his tablet, and lowered his voice. "Sir, we all love Joanna, but she's been late for everything this week. We should have Kelly rearrange—"

"Heaven's sake, Wesley." Mr. Slynt patted Wesley's arm. "Do whatever you think is best, but this is Linda's time."

"Of course." Wesley thumbed through his tablet and showed the screen to Aunt Linda. "We have some preliminary items to iron out before the party, Chef Linda. Would you mind taking a look?"

Grayson's eyes remained fixed on the girl. She wore a black skirt and stylish ankle-high boots, with a button-down white blouse. Her forest green eyes popped in contrast to a porcelain complexion and soft pink lips. Golden hair cascaded in silky waves over her shoulders, as if it had been hand-painted in that position.

Grayson tried not to stare. His jaw hung open.

The girl pulled out her smartphone and began to nonchalantly tap the screen. She gave a soft smile, hinting at perfect white teeth.

"We'll need vegan options, but no tofu," Wesley chattered away. "No bourbon or rum-based desserts either. Salads should be two-toned. Marketing would prefer you not serve a salad named after a famous person other than Mr. Slynt. Every dish on the menu should be uniquely branded to the Slynt experience—"

"Wesley, please!" Mr. Slynt guided Wesley away from Aunt Linda. "Chef Linda knows how to design a menu."

Aunt Linda smiled politely. "My agent passed along *all* of your wonderful suggestions, Wesley. Mr. Slynt, have you met my nephews?" She gestured to each of them. "Jason is the day manager for Something Suite this summer. This is Grayson, my all-star scooper, and my little bookworm Mason who in a few years we hope to fold into the family business, too."

"Yeah, our parents named us Jason, Grayson, and Mason," Grayson explained. "They pretty much hate us."

Nobody laughed.

Mr. Slynt smiled. "Charming." He strolled behind the pretty blond girl and placed his hands on her shoulders. "Chef Linda, I'd like to introduce you to my daughter Lucienne. Lucy is visiting for the month and just flew in from Paris. Say hello, Lucy."

"*Bonjour*," Lucy remarked without glancing up.

"Lucy, be polite." Slynt laughed awkwardly. "She's a little fatigued from jetlag."

"I understand completely," Aunt Linda said. "Lucy, I hope you'll join us in the kitchen for the tasting."

"I am not hungry," she said.

Grayson smiled at Lucy's lyrical French accent.

"Well, if you'd like some ice cream, a shake, a smoothie, don't hesitate to ask. My nephews are here to serve you."

"You got that right!" Grayson said.

Jason elbowed him in the ribs.

"Ow!"

Aunt Linda shot Grayson a disapproving glance as she crossed behind the counter. "Please, right this way everyone!"

Wesley continued to chatter as the group followed Aunt Linda into the kitchen. "Asian fusion is out. Italian is in, but nothing too heavy! In today's business climate you might start with soup, but nothing too *soupy*!"

After Slynt and his people disappeared with Aunt Linda and Mason, Lucy sighed and wandered to a lobby chair.

"Smooth!" Jason whispered. "Our parents must hate us? Why would you say that?"

"You say that *all* the time and usually people laugh!" Grayson whispered back.

"I say that to friends and family, not important bah-zillionaires like Alexander Slynt and his cute French daughter. Put your eyes back in your head, by the way."

"Was I that bad?"

"Could have been worse." Jason shrugged. "You could have told her about the freezer monster."

"I *did* see something in the..." Grayson shook his head. "Whatever. A girl like that wouldn't talk to a guy like me, anyway."

"You're setting yourself up for defeat." Jason patted his shoulder. "Play it cool."

"That's what I *thought* I was doing."

"Watch and learn." Jason clicked his ice cream scooper and dished out a scoop of French vanilla in a pink Something Suite cup. He stuck a pink plastic spoon on top and carried it around the counter toward Slynt's daughter.

"Pardonez-moi, mademoiselle. Vous voudrais du glace a vanille? C'est très delicious."

Lucy glanced up from her phone. Her perfect lips spread into an enormous smile. *"Merci beaucoup!"* She accepted the cup and tasted the ice cream. *"Mmm. Très bien! Parlez vous Francais?"*

"Seulment un peu." Jason pinched his fingers slightly apart to indicate "a little bit." Then he said, *"Je m'appelle Jason North. Beinvenue aux Etas Unis!"*

"Je m'appelle Lucienne!" Then Lucienne began to speak very fast, making goo-goo eyes at Grayson's older brother. Grayson clenched his jaw in annoyance. He had forgotten about Jason's four years of high school French.

Jason nodded with interest and periodically stated, *"Oui, oui, bein sûr."* Then finally, after a long bout of laughter between the two, Jason noticed a line forming and excused himself.

Grayson busily scooped two double Dutch chocolate cones as his brother slipped behind the register and rang up the order.

"I hate you," Grayson whispered. He handed the cones to two grateful customers. "What was she saying?"

"No clue. Something about the airport? She was going a little fast for me."

"Well, I hope you guys are very happy together."

Jason laughed. "Gimmie a break! She's *your* age. I was just softening her up for you. Listen, when she finishes that cup of ice cream, go offer to collect her trash for her."

"What am I, a garbage man?"

"This is food service," Jason said. "You're *less* than a garbage man. I'm going to head in back and take inventory now that things have slowed down. Come get me if you need help."

"I can handle it," Grayson said.

Jason paused as he backed through the kitchen door. "I meant with her."

"Ha, ha!"

"I'll keep my eyes peeled for freezer monsters!" Jason called out.

"It wasn't a monster, it was a man," Grayson muttered. He turned the silvery copper ice cream scooper over in his hand. The cool metal tickled Grayson's palm. "I know I'm not crazy," he whispered. Maybe he hadn't truly seen a freezer guy or a fire monster, but there was something really weird about the silver key that kept changing forms.

He glanced up and saw that Slynt's daughter had gotten up and started to cross the lobby.

"Hey wait!" he shouted.

She ignored him and headed toward the garbage and recycling bins near the Riverwalk exit.

"Lucy!" he said.

The girl turned. "Yes?"

"Can I take your garbage?"

Lucy glared from Grayson down to the pink cup in her hand. "I can handle it." Lucy tossed the cup in the recycling bin and headed through the sliding automatic doors, just as two dour-looking bald men entered, each dressed in matching gray suits and sporting dark black shades.

Grayson sighed. "That didn't go well."

The suited men made a beeline for Something Suite. Grayson greeted them. "Good afternoon, and welcome to Something Suite. Can I help you to indulge in a sweet treat to keep you cool this fine summer day?"

The men sized up Grayson, their heads and necks moving in perfect sync. "This is the one that the mage sensed?" the man on the right asked.

"Possibly," the left one said. "The signature is weaker now. It was strong before."

Grayson's ice cream scooper chilled in his hand. His breath puffed. His heartrate quickened. "You guys aren't here for ice cream, are you?"

"He is small. Quite young." The stranger on the left removed his shades, revealing bright, fiery eyes.

"Agreed." The one on the right removed his shades. His eyes also burned like torches. "But age makes no difference. Only his emotions make him worthy."

Both men's mouths stretched into perfectly circular O shapes. The flesh around their faces pulled back into accordion folds. Two horrible, twitching matchstick creatures with skin like magma revealed themselves.

Chapter 6

Grayson tensed and backed away from the counter. His first instinct was to scream, but his voice snagged in his throat.

"He cannot be the one!" the first creature's voice sizzled like hot coals. "We would sense it!"

"Fear of our Sulfurian forms may be suppressing his true nature," his companion grumbled. "We must touch him to be certain."

"Whoa!" Grayson held out his ice cream scooper. Icy air swirled around his limbs. A chill shot up his spine. "Keep your red-hot hands to yourselves!"

Grayson's breath steamed. A cocoon of ice coated his fist and formed a frozen hilt over the scooper. Then a long, sharp blade of ice stabbed toward the Sulfurians.

The creatures hissed and recoiled.

"Back off, you crispy creeps!" Grayson's heart surged with adrenaline. His fears evaporated.

The Sulfurians spread their claws. Tufts of orange fire sprouted in their palms. "It is he! The accursed Frost-Keeper! The key has been passed on!"

"You got that right!" Grayson shouted. "Now

scram! Don't make me use my ice cream-scoop-key-flashlight-sword-deally-thing on you!"

The two Sulfurians erupted with rage. Fire curled from their eyes. The flames on their hands exploded into bright yellow pillars. "Incinerate him!"

Grayson ducked as yellow-white fireballs blasted overhead. He tucked his ice blade at his side and crawled for cover.

The Sulfurians snaked their gangly torsos over the counter and spat fire at Grayson.

Grayson raised his sword in defense. Instantly, the blade widened into a thick shield of ice, blocking the fiery blasts. Grayson rolled toward the edge of the counter, leapt to his feet, and darted into the lobby. His ice shield slimmed back into a frozen sword. He charged the two Sulfurians.

The monsters' wrists elongated, as if they were made of elastic magma. Their claws sharpened into white-hot talons. The first one lunged and swiped at Grayson.

Grayson narrowly avoided the attacks. He counter-slashed and sliced off one of the creature's hands. The Sulfurian screamed. His hand crystallized into ice in midair and shattered when it hit the ground.

The one-handed monster lurched toward Grayson. His eyes exploded with molten fury. Grayson ducked, then instinctively stabbed upward. His ice-blade skewered the Sulfurian through the mouth. A blanket of frost enveloped the Sulfurian from his head down his alien torso to his human feet. The monster completely froze and exploded into a pile of snow.

The second Sulfurian's glowing face gaped at Grayson for a moment; then he made a mad dash toward the Riverwalk exit, phony human skin flapping behind him.

Instinct took over again. Instead of chasing the creature, Grayson aimed his sword, concentrated, and fired an arctic white beam of light across the lobby. Icy energy shot through the creature's back. Just like his partner, the Sulfurian's whole body froze, from the torso outward, crystallized, and exploded into frost. The white beam faded, leaving a slick coat of ice on the revolving glass door.

Grayson's ice sword swiftly melted back into the ordinary handle of his ice cream scoop. He collapsed onto his knees to catch his breath. "What! The heck! Was that!" he shouted.

His mind reeled with questions. *How did I just summon ice? Since when do I know how to swordfight? How did those creatures find me, and how many more are there?*

He glanced around the lobby. No hotel patrons or staff had been in view, but the front desk manager was rounding the corner to investigate the noise.

The kitchen door behind the Something Suite counter burst open. "Grayson!" Jason shouted. "What have you done?"

"What have *I* done?" Grayson's legs wobbled as he got back on his feet. He stepped right into the snowy remains of a dead Sulfurian. "Ew! Gross!"

"Grayson, I'm going to kill you!" Jason's face burned red with anger. He pulled a dripping tub of syrupy white liquid from the freezer. "All of this ice cream is melted! Do you have *any* idea how much product this is?"

"Hey! I'm fine!" Grayson snapped. "Thanks for asking!"

"What is going on here!" The front desk manager furrowed his brow at the carpet. "There's ice and snow everywhere! We just had this cleaned. What is that?" He rushed over to the revolving glass door and pressed against it. "This is *frozen* shut... on the *hottest* day of the summer!"

"Okay." Grayson was still struggling to catch his breath. "Give me a minute. I can explain... I think."

"Why would you throw freezer frost all over the carpet? Is this supposed to be a joke?" Jason demanded.

"Throw freezer frost?" Grayson shook his head at the Sulfurian remains. "There wasn't even that much frost *in* the freezer. Are you kidding me? Seriously, *nobody* saw any of what just happened?"

"We cannot have people shouting, making a mess, and... *freezing doors!*" the front desk manager shouted. "I don't care whose nephew you are, I will have you removed from this hotel!"

"Okay, hang on a second!" Grayson signaled for time-out with his ice cream scoop. "I have to show you something."

"Grayson," came Aunt Linda's stone-cold voice from the kitchen doorway. "In my office. Now!"

Mr. Slynt glared over her shoulder.

Grayson's heart thudded with panic. The room started to spin. "No, no, no. Please. I can explain. It's this!" He held up his ice cream scooper. "It's a sword or something. These things came and attacked."

"Gray," Jason whispered. "Stop it! You're losing your mind. You're going to get us *all* in trouble."

"But I can prove it!" Grayson held out his ice cream scooper. He concentrated. His hand trembled. He strained to focus. "Come on, sword," he whispered. "Don't leave me hanging."

Nothing happened.

"Grayson," Aunt Linda ordered. "In. My office.

Now!"

Two custodians approached the frosty piles with push brooms and dustpans.

"Okay," Grayson said. "But don't throw that stuff out. We need to get it tested in a lab or something. These guys are not human. They throw fireballs and—"

"Grayson! Shut up!" Jason snapped. "Just get back there."

Grayson's face burned with shame. He slowly rounded the counter. He could feel the angry stares of Jason, Aunt Linda, Mr. Slynt, and every member of his entourage who had gathered behind the kitchen door.

The stone-faced crowd parted, and Grayson made his way to Aunt Linda's office. As he closed the door, he heard Aunt Linda apologizing profusely. "I am so sorry, Mr. Slynt. I accept full responsibility for this. We will get to the bottom of..."

Grayson slumped in the office chair. He throttled the handle of his scooper. "Come on! Work! You're making me look like a complete psycho! I know I'm not..."

Grayson's eyes caught the glowing screen of the computer. On it, he could see Jason, desperately cleaning up the melted mess in the freezer case. The cleaning people were straightening out the lobby. Slynt's entourage was leaving. Wesley was emphatically pointing to items on his tablet agenda.

"I'm *not* crazy, because the security footage caught the whole thing!" Grayson smiled.

Chapter 7

"Grayson Bartholomew North!" Aunt Linda slammed the office door behind her. "What do you have to say for yourself?"

Grayson stood tall. He looked his aunt right in the eyes. "I'm innocent."

Aunt Linda's returning glare felt intense enough to drill a hole through his eyes.

"Or... I'm crazy?" Grayson gulped. "Personally, I'm hoping for innocent. But Aunt Linda, I swear to you—and I would not lie about something like this— two weird creatures walked into the lobby, came right up to the counter and spewed fire at me!"

"Oh my God." Aunt Linda's eyes drooped. She leaned against her desk for support. "You *are* crazy!"

"Review the security footage." Grayson tapped at the monitor. "How do you rewind?"

"That's a live feed, Grayson," Aunt Linda said. "Only Slynt Security can review footage. And they will. I don't want to fire you, but unless we can come up with a really good explanation for what you did and why you did it—"

"You won't have to fire me. Listen, all this weird

stuff started this morning. This guy followed me on the Red Line and gave me this key that turned into a flashlight that turned into a..." Grayson caught his aunt's glare again.

The more I explain, the crazier I sound, Grayson realized. "Just... wait for the footage, I guess. Why should anyone believe me?" He collapsed in the office chair.

"Grayson," Aunt Linda said. "I thought a part time job this summer would be a good thing for you. But maybe you're not mature enough."

Grayson clenched his jaw. His face burned with anger.

"You're young. There's a lot going on in your life. You have too much stress, and I guess I added to it."

"I *am* mature enough," Grayson pleaded. "And you're right. It *is* stressful when my own family thinks I'm crazy."

Aunt Linda's eyes melted into concern. "I don't know how to handle this, Gray. I don't know what's going on in your head. Are you lashing out because of your parents?"

Grayson's head throbbed with frustration. "This is *not* about my parents."

"You've always been excitable, but never destructive like this." Aunt Linda took a deep breath. She shook her head. "I need you to take the afternoon off. Just get out of the hotel, and I will do what I can to smooth this over."

"I'm really sorry about the ice cream, Aunt Linda," Grayson said. "But it was not me."

"This is not about ice cream, Grayson," she said.

A muffled sneeze interrupted the silence. Aunt Linda opened the office door, and Grayson's little brother tumbled into the room. "Mason!" Aunt Linda helped him to his feet. "Were you eavesdropping?"

Mason dusted himself off. "No, I swear. Jason wants to know if you want him to shut down the store while he cleans up. A line is forming."

"No! We stay open. I'll help him."

"I can help." Grayson stood.

"Absolutely not!" Aunt Linda pointed at him, as if the gesture could pin him to the chair. "Stay right there!" She hurried out front.

Mason stared at his brother. An awkward silence hung between them.

"Well?" Grayson shrugged. "Come to get a good look at your crazy brother?"

"Actually," Mason said. "I believe you."

"You... believe me?" Grayson smiled. "Seriously, Mace?"

Mason nodded.

Grayson's heart skipped a beat. Finally, someone didn't think he was crazy. "Why, though? I mean, *I* kinda don't believe me."

"The physics of it all," Mason said. "It doesn't make sense. There's more snow and ice in the lobby than you could have scraped off the freezer, and it would have taken a flame thrower to melt that much ice cream that fast. I mean, I don't know if it was a monster, but something weird for sure. Right?"

"Thanks, buddy!" Grayson held up his ice cream scooper. "I just wish this stupid Frost-Key would work again."

"Frost-Key?"

Grayson concentrated. His hands shook. "I swear, this turned into a sword made of ice. It shot this beam of arctic light across the lobby."

Mason shrugged. "If that's what happened, that's what the security footage will show, right?"

"Grayson!" Aunt Linda reappeared. "This is Mr. Cortez, head of Mr. Slynt's personal security."

The buff, bald man who had been part of Slynt's entourage loomed behind her. The man still wore dark shades in addition to his sleek tailored black suit. A Bluetooth headset was clipped to his ear.

Grayson held out his hand for shaking, but Cortez only glared, blank and unreadable. He presented a sleek chrome tablet. "Here is what just happened in the lobby," Cortez spoke in an imposing baritone.

Grayson's heart hammered. The full color video feed showed the scene from a few minutes ago. There was no audio, but Grayson watched himself calling out to Lucy Slynt. Lucy paused, glared at him, tossed her paper cup in the trash, and headed out the door.

The two creepy strangers entered the lobby. Then suddenly there was a strange flicker. The men paused. They appeared to be talking to each other, but far away from the counter.

"Wait," Grayson said. "Wait, this didn't happen."

The disguised Sulfurians took a right and proceeded toward the front desk.

"They didn't do that! They came right up to... Hey!"

Grayson watched in horror as his recorded-self turned and stared directly into the security camera. His video doppelganger grinned mischievously, tossed his ice cream scooper up and down a few times and then hurled it right at the screen. The camera jerked toward the wall. The rest of the feed stayed fixed on the upper corner of the shop—away from where the real action had occurred.

Chapter 8

"No. Way!" Grayson shook his head at the imposter in the recording. "That did *not* happen!"

"Grayson," Aunt Linda whispered. "Please be honest about this."

"I—"

"Young man!" Cortez tucked the tablet under his arm and adjusted his shades. "You need to understand that apart from vandalism, tampering with hotel security equipment is a very serious offense."

"Of course it is!" Grayson said. "That's why I would never—"

"You're a minor, your aunt is an important part of this hotel, and this is a first offense." Cortez leaned inches from Grayson's face. "So I am going to do you a huge, *huge* favor and let you off with a warning. Mr. Slynt and management does not need to know all of the details of this incident."

Grayson struggled for words. "I swear I—I…"

"The words you are looking for, Grayson, are 'Thank you.'" Aunt Linda's concrete stare drilled into him.

"Thank you," Grayson whispered.

"We are so, so sorry, Mr. Cortez." Aunt Linda folded her hands over her heart. She placed a hand on Grayson's shoulder. "Nothing like this will ever happen again. Right, Grayson?"

"No. Of course not." Grayson's heart sank. *It didn't happen the first time.*

"Grayson is suspended from work," Aunt Linda added, "until further notice. And he's grounded. And the cost of the damages is coming out of his paychecks."

Grayson squeezed his fists. Tears welled in his eyes.

"Mr. Cortez," Mason spoke up. "What was that blip?"

The man tilted his head extra far down at Mason. "Blip?"

"After those two people walked in. There was a blip. Like the movie jumped or something."

"Feedback."

"It looked like someone edited the footage," Mason said.

"I saw it, too." Grayson tried not to sniffle. Tears leaked down his cheeks.

Cortez laughed. "This isn't Hollywood. If the security camera showed you vandalizing hotel property, then that is exactly what happened."

"But it didn't show everything," Mason said. "How did the ice cream melt? Where did all that snow come from?"

Cortez adjusted his shades. "Ask the vandal. I don't have time for this. Good day, Chef Linda." Cortez tucked his tablet under his arm and marched through the kitchen.

"Aunt Linda—" Grayson started.

"I can't deal with this, right now, Gray. I have five hundred things to do for Slynt's engagement party. Jason is dealing with a complete disaster in the lobby. And not only have you embarrassed our family, but you're also making me worried sick."

"Someone faked that footage!"

"Enough!" Aunt Linda shouted. "I'm getting you a cab, and you're going home. Stay at my condo and think about what you've done. When I get home, we'll talk."

"Grayson was supposed to take me to the history museum," Mason reminded her. "It's not fair to punish both of us, right?"

"Mason, this is—" She shook her head, sighed. "All right, fine. But after Mason is done at the museum, you're both going straight home. I'm checking with the doorman, and he better have seen you by five o'clock."

She grabbed her purse off the table. "Here's money for admission." She handed Mason two twenty dollar bills. "Bring me my change. Don't forget your transit cards. Leave your phones on. I want you both to check in."

"Thank you, Aunt Linda," Mason said.

"Keep a close eye on your brother," she said.

"I will," Grayson said.

Aunt Linda glared. "I was talking to Mason." She hurried through the kitchen.

Mason turned toward him. "Cortez was lying."

"Tell me about it, brother." Grayson gave a weak smile. "Thanks, Mace. At least someone in this family has my back."

"I read this book on the telltale signs of liars," Mason continued. "Liars always fidget. Did you see how he kept adjusting his sunglasses? Liars also deflect accusations. When I asked questions, he just responded with *different* questions. And he was in such a hurry to leave."

"But how could they edit that footage so fast? Even I have to admit it sounds impossible." Grayson shook his head.

"Fast editing technology is actually pretty plausible, compared to an ice-sword and fire monsters."

"Good point." Grayson examined the security monitor on the office desk again. Jason was hard at work fixing a sundae. "Why would Slynt's security cover this up?"

Cortez's bald face flashed in Grayson's mind. He pictured him adjusting his sunglasses. "Oh no!" The redhead in the subway, the two Sulfurians that Grayson had fought in the lobby. They had all worn shades.

"We need to get out of here." Grayson tugged his brother by the wrist and dragged him through the shop door. Jason handed a sundae to a customer, then shot Grayson a hateful glance.

"Grayson," Jason said. "Come here."

Grayson glanced furtively around the lobby for suspicious characters wearing sunglasses. The coast was clear. "Mace, wait outside. I'll be right there." He approached Jason.

"When I get home tonight, you and I are having a long, long talk."

"Why," Grayson said. "You're not Dad, you know."

"Thank God for that," Jason snapped.

Grayson scowled. "You know something, Jason? Dad trusts me. Dad likes me. And I wish he were here instead of you."

Jason's eyes burned. "Get out of here, before I

really lose my temper."

Grayson turned back around to find Mason, standing next to the counter, listening to their exchange. He ushered his little brother along. "Come on. Let's go."

Grayson's guts tightened. He could feel Jason's angry glare on the back of his head as they crossed the lobby. *Why oh why, on top of dealing with Aunt Linda, and Slynt's suspicious security guy, do I have to take garbage from you, Jason?* he wondered. *I have bigger problems.*

He ushered Mason through the revolving doors. The midday sun blazed. July heat swelled around them. Grayson led his brother down the stone steps to the blue-green ripples of the Chicago River. "I didn't want to talk in there because if that security guy is no good, the whole place could be bugged. But I have a really bad feeling, Mason. I want you to stay close to me today, okay?"

Mason hesitated. "Okay."

"I saw a lady in the transit tunnel today. She wore dark sunglasses, and when she took them off, her eyes burned like fire. The things in the lobby were the same. These creatures, the Sulfurians, wear fake human skin, but they still have to hide the fire in their eyes in order to blend in."

Grayson surveyed the Riverwalk. Tourists, boat guides, and other pedestrians were out in full force. Half of them wore shades or dark glasses.

"Cortez wears sunglasses indoors," Mason said. "I figured he was just trying to look tough. You think he's one of these Sulfurians?"

"That's just one thing I need help figuring out." Grayson placed his hand on his brother's shoulder. "Do you seriously believe I'm not crazy?"

Mason nodded.

"Good." Grayson took a deep, calming breath. When he exhaled, frosty air, cooled his lips. He pulled his ice cream scooper from his pocket. Cold air swirled up his arm. He flicked his wrist, and the icy Frost-Key changed into the Frost-Blade. He raised his sword triumphantly. "There we go!"

Mason's eyes grew wild with excitement.

"I knew I could do it!" Grayson's breath puffed into a white cloud. "You are seeing this, right?"

"You're not crazy," Mason said. "And I will totally help you!"

"Mace, you are my favorite brother." Grayson retracted the icy blade back into the scooper. A freezing aura still surrounded him, like an air-conditioned cocoon.

"What's that?" Mason pointed to the ground.

Grayson glanced down. An ice arrow curved along the concrete. "Huh. I guess it wants us to go that way." Grayson scratched his head. "What's that way?"

"North," Mason said. "The museum is north. That's where we're going anyway, right?"

Grayson nodded. "Good enough for me. Ready for an adventure?"

Chapter 9

Grayson and Mason caught the Red Line train toward the Clark and Division stop. Grayson scrutinized every suspicious commuter in shades. *Why did sunglass-wearing monsters have to attack on the sunniest day of July?* he wondered.

On the train, he filled his brother in on the details of his three encounters: the CTA tunnel, the freezer cave, and the hotel lobby. Mason nodded with interest as he accessed the Wi-Fi on his tablet. "There's nothing about Sulfurians online," Mason said.

"Makes sense," Grayson said. "Considering every person who meets one probably gets incinerated. But they always attack when I'm alone. And come to think of it, it's pretty weird to have the train tunnel and the Slynt lobby so empty in the middle of a Saturday."

"They must be afraid to reveal themselves in public," Mason said.

"Look up the name Victor Drake, Mace. Any info about my freezer buddy?"

Mason ran a search. He shook his head. "There's a

lot of people with that name, but none of them are Frost-Keepers. From the way you described his clothes, it sounds like he got frozen way before online records."

The frosty energy of Grayson's scooper cooled his pocket. "What about transforming keys and hidden freezer caves?"

"There's a lot about pocket dimensions and stuff," Mason said.

"There is?"

"Sure." Mason shrugged. "From made-up stories in books and movies."

Grayson sighed. "This key better be leading us to answers."

The two brothers exited the train and ascended into the oppressive July sunshine. When Grayson pulled the scooper from his pocket, a refreshing aura of air-conditioning swirled around them.

"How are you controlling the air like that?" Mason asked. "It's awesome!"

"It just sort of happens on autopilot."

"Hey, Gray? Can I try?" Mason nodded at the ice cream scooper in Grayson's hand.

"Sure, just be careful." Grayson handed his brother the scooper. Immediately, hot, muggy air collapsed in on them. The pleasant chill in Grayson's limbs vanished, and he started to sweat.

Mason flipped the scooper over. He swiped the air, but nothing happened. "I wonder why it only works for you?"

"Victor said it chose me as the 102nd Frost-Keeper." Grayson accepted the scooper back from his brother. Arctic air swirled around them.

A passing stranger shivered in confusion.

"I wonder how cold I can make it?" Grayson

whispered. He concentrated. An arctic breeze swept down Clark Street. Every pedestrian reacted in surprised refreshment. People smiled in unexpected joy at the arrival of the impossibly cold gust of air.

Grayson focused, and the temperature dropped further. Ice crystals crept over his fingers and dripped down the handle of the scooper.

Mason rubbed his bare arms. "Gray," he whispered.

"Isn't this cool?" Grayson marveled.

"Yeah, but look!" Mason pointed to Grayson's feet. A patch of ice spread from the soles of his shoes. "You're drawing attention."

Grayson lost his focus. The chill in the air dissipated. The ice at his feet began to melt. People were staring. "Come on." He tugged his brother up the street toward the museum.

That was dumb, Grayson thought. *Half those people were wearing shades. What if I just revealed us to more Sulfurians?* "Stay close, buddy," he told his brother. "If you notice anyone wearing shades indoors, tell me, okay?"

Mason nodded.

The Chicago History Museum was a long, brown-brick building with a round glass rotunda at one end. Huge banners draped over the entrance, advertising special exhibits on Al Capone, Prohibition, and the evolution of the skyscraper.

A spacious lobby featured an old-fashioned automobile, neon signs from the 1920s, and huge black and white murals of Chicago throughout the decades. Mason marveled at the collection of street signs that dangled from the ceiling while Grayson paid admission.

They headed up a spiral staircase through an

expansive walkthrough that explained the city's development from pioneer days to modern times.

A life-sized reconstruction of an original El Train and platform served as the main exhibit's centerpiece. Other train engines and vehicles were prominently displayed in the wide open space. Mason rushed from one exhibit to the next, eagerly studying each plaque.

Meanwhile, an icy buzz in Grayson's pocket distracted him. *What now?* he wondered. Was his Frost-Key trying to warn him about something? He sized-up the other patrons but didn't spot any shady characters.

"Wow!" Mason studied a corner display. "These are original correspondences from the Civil War!"

Grayson stood behind him. He strained his eyes to read the tight, squiggly script of the yellowing papers. "Honestly, unless this letter says something about why I inherited a magic ice cream scooper, I'm not that interested."

Mason sighed. "But, Gray, if there *is* information, we won't find it unless we actually *read* the documents. Maybe we should split up."

"No," Grayson said. "You didn't see what those Kentucky-fried creatures can do. Stick with me and be safe."

"It could take forever to find what we're looking for. This is a big museum."

Grayson surveyed the exhibits. "Maybe that ice arrow didn't even mean for us to—" A familiar sight sent chills down Grayson's spine. "Here we go!" He rushed toward another display; his brother hurried after him.

Inside, a mannequin wore a blue uniform and a sturdy metal helmet. Badges, axes, tools, and equipment, along with rubber gloves and boots, were prominently displayed beneath the caption: *Chicago Fire Department Uniform circa 1890.*

"Victor Drake wore an outfit a lot like this!" Grayson said. "He was a firefighter! In more ways than one, I guess."

"Uh... Grayson..." Mason pointed at the display behind them: a wall of information on The Great Chicago Fire. Photographs, drawings, models, maps, and article clippings chronicled the devastation.

"Whoa!" Grayson said. "Victor Drake wasn't just a firefighter and Frost-Keeper. He lived through the Great Chicago Fire."

Mason read the plaque. "'The fires burned for three days, from Sunday October eighth through Tuesday October tenth, 1871.' This was one of the biggest natural disasters in the history of America! What if..."

Grayson locked eyes with his brother. "You don't think..."

"If Victor Drake was a fireman around 1890, he could have been about your age when the Great Fire happened. Maybe the Sulfurians started the whole thing the last time they attacked?"

Grayson pointed to a drawing labeled *O'Leary Farm*, which showed a spotted cow kicking a fiery lantern. "But everyone knows a stupid cow caused the fire. Not Sulfurian monsters."

Mason groaned. "Read the plaque, Gray! It says right here: 'The story of Mrs. O'Leary's cow has become a popular legend but has never been confirmed.' Whatever really started the fire, it was flammable building materials, dry weather, and wind that helped it spread."

Grayson scanned the articles and clippings in the

display for more info. "This is all really interesting, Mace, but I kinda don't think it's going to say anything about Sulfurians or magic keys. Maybe we should check the library or town records or something? If we can find more about Victor Drake—"

A hand clutched Grayson's shoulder. Someone yanked him around, and he gasped.

The redhead from the tunnel, Scarlett Fury, loomed over him. She clenched his shoulders. Her sunglasses slipped down the bridge of her nose, revealing blazing yellow light. "Nice cold front out there, kid. Led me *right* to you."

Grayson reached into his pocket, but the woman's fingertips glowed like hot coals. Pain crippled Grayson. Smoke rose from his singed t-shirt.

Scarlett Fury laughed. Flames licked the back of her throat. "Your career is over before it's begun, Frost-Keeper. Prepare to burn!"

Chapter 10

"**H**elp!" Mason shouted. "This crazy lady is attacking my brother!" Every patron in the exhibit was now staring in their direction. Two security guards bolted across the room.

"Another chore for the mages!" Scarlett Fury huffed. "I *was* only going to kill *you*, Frost-Keeper. But if I must burn this whole museum to ash, so be it!"

Grayson blocked out the searing pain of the woman's red-hot fingertips on his shoulder. He inhaled, held his breath, and felt his lungs freeze. Then he exhaled a blast of subzero air. Frost sprayed over Scarlett Fury's face. Icicles stabbed through her auburn locks. She growled and stumbled backwards.

"Run, Mason!" Grayson drew his ice cream scooper as Mason darted into the adjacent wing.

The security guards approached. "Step away from him, ma'am!"

Scarlett Fury snarled. Tufts of fire blazed on her palms. The guards backed away, startled. She lurched forward to scorch them.

"Get back!" Grayson pointed his scooper at the

floor, and a patch of ice slicked under Scarlett's high heels. She slipped and crashed.

The two guards stared in stunned silence as frosty vapors poured from Grayson's mouth. He pointed with his scooper toward the exit. "Evacuate the museum. I'll stop her."

Hot air billowed from the floor, and the Sulfurian floated to her feet.

Grayson flicked his wrist, and the Frost-Blade stabbed out of the scooper.

The two guards exchanged incredulous looks, then snapped into action. They shouted to the crowd and directed people toward the stairs.

Waves of heat undulated from the woman, warped the air. Grayson's air-conditioned cocoon chilled to compensate.

Scarlett Fury stalked forward; tongues of fire sprouted from her footfalls. "Make no mistake, boy, the drones you slaughtered at the hotel were candle fumes." Her skin peeled back, revealing the twitching monster inside. "I am Scarlett Fury!"

Grayson raised an eyebrow. "Who?"

"Scarlett Fury!" she snapped. "Warrior Class Elite! Stewardess of the Supreme Sulfurian Collective! And I will not be so easily vanquished by—"

Grayson whipped a snowball between her eyes. "You talk a lot, Scarlett Fury!"

Scarlett's face glowed like a jack-o'-lantern, instantly sublimating the snowball into steam. Claws extended into white-hot daggers. Smoke billowed from her pores.

Fire alarms blared. The sprinkler system sprayed jets of water that shrouded the Sulfurian inferno in steam.

Grayson swiped and thrust his Frost-Blade, but

Scarlett dodged each attack. She countered with a double dose of blazing fireballs. Grayson deflected them with his sword; white light flashed against the display cases.

For a moment, Grayson's reflection in the glass startled him. Water from the sprinklers had frozen to his face and chest, coating him in translucent white. His hair spiked in frosty spires.

Scarlett hurled another molten blast, and Grayson deflected it against the case. Glass melted like lava. Vintage newspapers, historic clothes, and other artifacts burned.

"That stuff is priceless you know!" Grayson snapped. "No respect for history!" With his free hand, Grayson sprayed white frost to salvage the artifacts.

The twitching matchstick creature glowed brighter, hotter. "This city will soon *become* history!" Her jagged mouth spewed fire.

Grayson's blade widened into a shield. He held his ground until the stream of fire subsided. Once he had an opening, he hardened his shield into a frozen battering ram and shoved it forward. He unleashed a pulse of icy energy that knocked the Sulfurian clear across the exhibit. She hit the metal guardrail and crashed through the opening of the reconstructed El Train.

Grayson rushed after her, Frost-Blade ready. Scarlett Fury sprang to her feet and hurled flaming projectiles through the train. Grayson deflected each fireball, but the wooden passenger benches of the exhibit caught fire.

The Sulfurian screamed an inhuman noise that rattled Grayson's ears. The interior of the train car glowed white and erupted. Grayson's sword swirled back into a shield and blocked the brunt of the explosion. Shockwaves sent him hurtling through the air onto his back.

Alarms blared. Black smoke crawled along the ceiling.

The train platform was now a black shadow, glowing with fire. Grayson morphed his shield back into a sword. He aimed the blade at the blazing El Train. A beam of arctic energy blasted into the exhibit and snuffed out the flames. Steam and white smoke billowed from the windows of the train's burnt out husk.

Grayson searched the room. Scarlett Fury had disappeared. The sprinklers extinguished lingering traces of fire, and most of the museum's artifacts remained safe behind glass. Grayson used his Frost-Blade to put out some of the stronger blazes. Then he heard coughing nearby.

He raced to a nook of the exhibit and found Mason huddled in the corner, gagging on the smoke. Mason's eyes watered. He coughed into his shirt.

Grayson helped his brother to his feet and steered him out of the exhibit. They rushed to an emergency exit toward the back of the second story. Grayson pushed his way out the door. Mason clutched the metal balcony and gagged. Smoke poured from the doorway.

Grayson summoned a rush of cold air that momentarily cleared the smoke. Mason inhaled a deep, cleansing breath.

"You okay, Mace?" Grayson examined his brother.

Mason nodded. He was breathing comfortably. His eyes were clear.

Sirens blared in the distance.

Grayson suddenly had a bad feeling about all the questions the authorities would have for him. "Let's

get away from here, Mace. I need to clear my head."
He led his brother down the fire escape. Summer air
melted the frost off his hair and face. Water dripped
down his forehead.

They rounded the corner. A crowd had gathered in
front of the museum. Fire engines and squad cars
swarmed the intersection of North and Clark.
Grayson's heart hammered. *Should we tell them
what we know?* he wondered. *Would they believe me?
Would it only put more people in danger, like Victor
warned?* His ice cream scooper sent a chill up his
wrist.

Mason tugged his shirt, and Grayson glanced
down. The scooper had made another ice arrow on the
sidewalk, but it was clearly pointing southeast now,
in the opposite direction as the disturbance.

"I don't think your sword wants us to stay here,"
Mason said. "Besides, what if that fire lady is still
watching?"

Grayson nodded. "Keep your head down. Stick with
me." They walked up North Avenue toward Lake
Michigan. "What if the police blame me for what
happened?"

"I don't think anyone got a good look at you,"
Mason said. "Except that Sulfurian lady."

"What do you mean?"

"There was so much steam from your breath. Then
when the sprinklers went off, all that water froze to
your face. It was like a mask, I bet. They only saw
her."

Grayson leaned on his knees as vertigo overcame
him.

Mason stared, wide-eyed. "Gray, are you okay?"

"Oh yeah, no prob." He struggled for a breath.
"Everything's cool. I just battled a fire-demon in the

Chicago History Museum and nearly got us killed." His voice cracked. "No big deal."

"Grayson!" Mason placed a hand on Grayson's shoulder. "You saved me. You saved all the people in that building. You extinguished the fire and saved the museum!" A huge smile spread across his brother's face. Grayson couldn't recall the last time he'd seen his brother smile so big. "My brother is a superhero! This is the coolest thing that's ever happened to me!"

Grayson's chest swelled with pride. Air swirled and chilled around him again. "When you put it like that, I guess it could've gone worse."

"It was awesome!" Mason said.

"Glad you think so, but it would be more awesome if I understood this whole Frost-Keeper thing a little better."

Mason opened his tablet case. "I hope this didn't get water or smoke damaged." He carefully examined the casing and hit the power button. The tablet powered up. "Yes!"

Grayson pushed the tablet back into Mason's case. "I am all about resuming the research, buddy," he said. "But somewhere quiet and out of the way. Let's get some lunch and figure out our next move."

Grayson glanced over his shoulder as they hurried toward Lake Michigan. The museum crowd had grown larger. By the bus stop, a bearded man wearing sunglasses checked his phone. Two women in shades sat in the front seat of a convertible, stopped at a red light. Everywhere, it seemed, pedestrians with dark eyewear lurked.

Any one of them, Grayson feared, could be a disguised Sulfurian.

Chapter 11

Grayson and Mason ducked into a lakeside restaurant by North Avenue Beach. Grayson scrutinized the crowds of sunglass-wearing beachgoers out the window. He hated that any one of them could be a fire-spewing monster, but somehow, he felt safe.

It's the water, something in the back of his head told him. The Frost-Key chilled his pocket. *There's something right about being close to the lake.*

"When the sprinklers went off back at the museum, it kinda helped," Grayson told his brother. "My ice powers sucked in the moisture, made me stronger."

"Makes sense." Mason pulled out his tablet. "Ice is frozen water, so to use your powers, your scooper probably freezes nearby gas or liquid water molecules."

"It's not really a scooper, Mace. The Frost-Key just disguises itself as a—" Grayson pulled the object from his pocket. The silvery-copper object had converted back to flashlight form. "Flashlight now, apparently."

"I wonder how it switches shapes." Mason rubbed

his chin.

"Victor called it adaptanium. It's a special metal that always stays the same size and weight, perfect for a sword handle." He pocketed the flashlight.

Suddenly, the restaurant quieted as a news report unfolded on a wall-mounted screen: "… *flames were extinguished, and fortunately, nobody was injured. Representatives from the Chicago History Museum and the Chicago Fire Department have informed us that a gas leak was likely responsible.*"

Grayson leapt to his feet. His chair clattered behind him. "Gas leak? Um, no!"

"*The investigation is ongoing,*" the reporter continued, "*but we're told the damage to the exhibit is not extensive. At this time, no word on when the museum will reopen to the public. Back to you, Ron!*"

"What a load of Mrs. O'Leary's cow crud!" Grayson snapped.

"Gray!" Mason whispered. "Sit down. People are staring."

"Oh. Heh." Grayson sheepishly picked up his chair. "I just… I loved that museum." He leaned closer to his brother and whispered, "How come nobody mentioned the Sulfurian fire-monster or the ice-wielding hero?"

"I thought you didn't want them to know it was you."

"I didn't want them to know it was Grayson North. But I'm fine with the Frost-Keeper taking credit. This makes no sense. Those security guards got an up-close look at both Scarlett Fury and the Frost-Keeper in action!" Grayson groaned. "If the news would just report what *actually* happened, then maybe Jason and Aunt Linda would believe—"

Grayson frowned. "Oh my God! Aunt Linda!" He

pulled his phone out of his pocket to discover five missed calls and a dozen texts.

Don't go to the museum! Go straight home.

Call me right away!

Where are you!

"Shoot!" Grayson hit the call button, and Aunt Linda picked up immediately.

"Grayson!"

"Hey, Aunt Linda, sorry, sorry, super sorry, but we're both okay! Mason and I actually didn't go right to the museum. We got delayed and saw a bunch of firetrucks, so we got lunch instead."

"Oh, thank God!" Aunt Linda said. "They said nobody was hurt, but still, I'm glad you're both okay."

"Don't worry; we're fine," Grayson assured her. "And I'm sorry about everything that happened today. It'll all make sense soon, I promise."

There was a long pause, and then Aunt Linda said. "What happened today?"

"You know," Grayson said. "The incident with security. Melted ice cream."

"Oh, that's not your fault, Gray," she said. "The freezer malfunctioned."

Grayson paused. "No, it didn't."

"Sure it did. I'm filing a claim with the manufacturer. Listen, stay safe in the city today. If you want to earn extra hours in the kitchen tonight, I could use help with Slynt's engagement party."

"I thought I was supposed to go straight home," Grayson said. "Aren't I suspended?"

"What's that? Hang on a second, Gray…" In the background, one of her kitchen staff lamented about a soufflé.

Grayson covered the phone and whispered to his brother. "Something's wrong. She's acting like she forgot about the whole lobby incident!" He pulled the phone back to his ear. "Aunt Linda, I need you to tell me what you remember about—"

"Gray, I'm so busy! Be safe. Touch base with me or Jason. By seven o'clock, I want you at my condo or with us at the hotel." The call ended.

"Just when I think this day can't get weirder," Grayson whispered. "Someone covered up the museum attack, and now Aunt Linda doesn't even remember the me-being-crazy version of the hotel attack. She thinks the freezer broke." Grayson shook his head. "Scarlett Fury said something at the museum: 'Another chore for the mages.' She mentioned mages in the Red Line tunnel, too."

Mason raised an eyebrow. "Who are the mages?"

"Don't know, but Victor Drake said Sulfurians can manipulate people's minds. We know they can change security footage, alter evidence in a flash. They must have done the same thing at the museum."

Grayson sighed. "I think Aunt Linda and Jason— maybe everyone at the Slynt Hotel—is in danger. I should go back and try to explain again. I'm getting a better handle on my powers. Once they see what I can do—"

"If you show off your powers at the hotel, you might only draw attention," Mason said. "Plus, if they control minds, they can make Aunt Linda and Jason forget again."

"I can't keep this from Aunt Linda. I'd be the worst nephew ever."

"Superheroes don't always tell their families about their powers, Gray. Maybe she's safer if she doesn't know."

"But Mace, the bad guys already saw my face. And

it's not like I didn't already blab to my little brother."

"I don't think we know enough about what's going on yet," Mason said. "There's no info online about Victor Drake. No clear connection between Sulfurians and the Chicago Fire. Search results for that lady's name—Scarlett Fury—only bring up lipstick and cosmetics. You bested her last time, but what if we go back to the hotel and *five* Scarlett Furies ambush you?"

"Good point," Grayson said. "Scarlett is way tougher than those Halloween rejects from the lobby. I got lucky."

"No way," Mason insisted. "You were awesome, Gray! You can totally take her!"

Grayson smiled. Steam spiraled from his mouth. "Yeah, I was pretty awesome."

"You just need practice."

"Practice? I know what I'm doing, look." Grayson discretely touched his fingertip to his drinking glass. The water froze solid. A giant crack split the glass. "Oops."

"When superheroes first test their new powers," Mason explained, "they go someplace to train."

"Where?" Grayson scoured the beach. "It's Saturday in July. Downtown Chicago is packed with tourists. And I don't think Aunt Linda would appreciate it if I accidentally turned her condo into an igloo."

"There's plenty of space." Mason pointed past the crowd at the swirling, crashing waves of Lake Michigan. "Out there."

"It's a lake." Grayson said. "It's not like we can rent a jet ski."

Mason smiled. "Why rent one, when you can *be* one?"

Chapter 12

After lunch, Grayson and Mason found a secluded area by the marina, away from beachgoers.

Grayson stared at the handle of his Frost-Key, now back in ice cream scoop form. Then he glanced down the wooden dock, over the rippling surface of Lake Michigan. Gulls cawed, and boats rocked between uneven waves. "I don't know, man."

"You can do it, Gray! Remember when you iced the sidewalk? It'll be like that, but on the water."

"You want me to make an ice... surfboard?" Grayson scratched his head.

"The lake is a limitless supply of water," Mason said. "If you get enough speed going, you can slide right across the surface. Get out far enough, and you can practice your powers away from people."

"Well, I am good at sliding down things," Grayson admitted.

"You are! Remember when Dad took us skiing and you went down the advanced slope? You were almost as good as Jason."

"Almost, huh?" Grayson emptied his pockets. He handed his wallet and phone to his brother. He looked around to make sure the coast was clear. Workers were tying up boats a few piers down, but they didn't seem to be paying attention.

Grayson got into a sprinting stance. "Wish me luck, Mace!" He bolted down the dock. The hilt of his blade froze over his fist. As he neared the edge of the dock, the Frost-Blade sprouted. He leapt toward the water and fired an arctic beam at the surging waves.

Grayson crashed through swirling, ice-cold water and plummeted deep down. He kicked frantically toward the surface and gasped for air. His clothes were soaked. Water froze in chunks all around him. Icicles dripped off his forehead.

Mason sheepishly smiled at the edge of the dock. "Didn't work, huh?"

"Not really, Mace, no!" Grayson aimed the tip of his sword toward his kicking feet. A solid block of ice formed beneath him and lifted him to the surface like an elevator. Grayson balanced himself on his ice floe. His wet clothes and skin turned frosty white.

"Well, you were right about one thing." Grayson aimed his sword. A narrow bridge of ice sprouted from his ice floe further into the lake. "It is easy to use my powers on the water. But not sure about this human jet ski thing."

"You need momentum," Mason said. "A jet ski has an engine that pushes it through the water. You can make ice and cold without the sword, right? You can make it on any part of your body, or anywhere nearby."

Grayson focused and a snowball congealed on his left palm. "Yep." He tossed the snowball at his brother's face.

"Hey!" Mason wiped his glasses on his shirt.

"That's for making me jump in the lake."

"You jumped in the lake on your own. Besides, I still think it'll work. Use this ice bridge as your runway. This time, aim your sword forward to create a path, but use the other hand to push yourself with an ice blast from behind."

Grayson climbed back onto the dock. "Worth a try, I guess." He walked back down the dock and motioned for Mason to step aside. Then he sprinted and took another running jump. He landed on the icy strip and slid toward open water. Waves lapped around his ankles.

Grayson aimed his sword forward and held his left palm behind him. A blast of super cold air fired out of his fingertips and propelled him along the frozen strip. Then he fired an icy beam from the Frost-Blade at the surface of the lake.

The bridge extended. Grayson rocketed forward.

Grayson shot like a frozen bullet. Frost sprayed behind him as he carved through the crashing waves. "Woo hoo!" He glanced back at his icy trail, breaking apart and swiftly melting away.

Nice, he thought. *My ice surfing is strong enough to support me, but not a danger to boats. The water is warm enough to melt my trail, too!*

Grayson increased the intensity of his blast trail and picked up speed. In the distance, boaters, skiers, and tubers stared and pointed. Grayson shot further across the lake away from people.

The skyline grew distant. He slowed down, slashed his sword, and created a wide ice floe to slide onto. Then he stabbed the Frost-Blade down to stop himself.

Grayson cheered. "Coolest thing I have *ever* done!"

He could barely make out his brother on the edge of the dock waving his arms. Grayson waved back.

He surveyed the surrounding waters. No boaters or swimmers nearby. The perfect opportunity to practice.

He spun his Frost-Blade. A sturdy ice shield swirled into his other hand. He practiced a few thrusts and parries, blocking imaginary attacks.

Grayson's shield melted. He gripped the handle of his sword with both hands and concentrated. The sword morphed and twisted into an ax, a club, a spear, then back into the lightweight sabre-shape it had first taken.

Other weapons might come in handy, he thought, *but the regular Frost-Blade is pretty maneuverable. Must be a reason it first formed this way.*

Grayson tested the power and range of his ice beams. He eyeballed the frosty patches he cast against distant waves and guessed his projectiles were most effective within fifty feet.

Grayson examined his frosty white arms and legs. *It's cool that I can frost over my face and clothes, but I'll bet I can make this icy coating stronger and thicker.*

Grayson concentrated. Thick ice plating covered his arms, legs, and chest. He sprouted spikey armored crystals on his shoulders, elbows, and knees. Protective ice head gear froze around his forehead and chin. "Nice!"

He glanced back at shore to find Mason frantically waving both arms. Grayson started to wave back. Then he noticed it. A black cloud billowed behind the marina. Smoke and fiery embers twisted into the sky.

The Sulfurians were heading right for his brother.

"Mason!" Suddenly, a large wave tilted Grayson's ice floe. The weight of his frozen armor threw him off balance, and Grayson slipped. He attempted to grab the surface of the floe, but his icy arms had no traction.

Water gushed over the ice and pushed him into the lake.

The armor on his limbs melted and broke apart underwater. He struggled toward the surface. *Don't panic,* he thought. *Make another ice-lift and—*

Grayson aimed his hands toward his feet, and then realized with horror: He had dropped the Frost-Key!

He frantically kicked until he surfaced.

"No, no, please, no!" Grayson floundered and searched around him. He struggled to see over the swelling waves, but he couldn't make out Mason or the dock, only the thickening cloud of smoke.

"Please don't be lost, please!" He dunked his head underwater but could only see darkness. The bottom of the lake had to be far below. And the key was pure metal.

Grayson swam toward the edge of his ice floe, praying that the scooper had miraculously landed on the platform. He struggled with his normal un-frosted hands to climb onto the ice, but it was too slippery.

Another swell of water rocked the ice floe up, and it slapped down on top of him. An undercurrent sucked Grayson beneath the ice. His body pressed against the frozen platform. Water went up his nose. He gagged.

Mason needs you! he thought. *Get out! Find that key!*

He twisted, kicked, and struggled until he popped up on the opposite side of the floe. Then he hacked up lake water, until he could finally get a breath.

"Help!" Grayson shouted. "Help! Anybody!"

Grayson spotted a tall, jagged shape, gently

bobbing between the waves. A perfect ice crystal.

"Yes!" The ice cream scooper was frozen in the middle of a miniature floating glacier.

Grayson frantically swam toward it. "Thank God, you have a failsafe!" He threw his arms around the icy buoy. The crystal automatically melted open to allow him access to the handle. As soon as Grayson grabbed it, ice crusted back over his skin. His powers rushed through his limbs, refreshing him like ice water on a hot day.

A new platform froze under Grayson's feet and bobbed him back to the surface. *Good news,* he thought. *My weapon likes me and doesn't want to get lost. Bad news: If someone takes it away, I'm pretty much helpless.*

Grayson froze another runway into the lake, took a running sprint, and rocketed toward the dock. He made out Mason shouting and pointing. The smoke was thicker, darker. A fiery glow appeared over the trees behind the Marina.

"Mason! Run! Get away from—" A powerful force knocked Grayson off his ice board, and he skidded across the waves. Grayson gripped the hilt of the Frost-Blade and kept it frozen between his fingers as he slowed and sank.

Fiery streaks glowed above the rippling surface of the water. Something circled the air. A creature, shadowed by flame, soared on enormous bat wings.

Chapter 13

Grayson floated to the surface on an ice floe. Armor froze over his torso. His shield swirled into his left hand.

"Frost-Keeper!" came a deep, smoky voice. The circling creature glowed white hot. "You are pathetic! Like an insect to flame!"

The creature slowed, spread his enormous bat wings, and hovered. White flames licked away to reveal a winged Sulfurian. Cracks and fissures glowed in his charcoal skin. The huge leathery wings, Grayson realized, were actually the Sulfurian's phony human skin stretched into flying appendages.

"Flying Sulfurians?" Grayson groaned. "Like you guys weren't annoying enough!"

"I am Blood-Wing!" the monster snarled. "Waif Commander and servant to his Omnipotent Volcanic Excellency!"

"Blood-Wing? Waif Commander?" Grayson shook his head. "Did these names come from a list of rejected action movies?"

Blood-Wing roared. "Prepare to melt beneath my

burning rage!" The Sulfurian's charred mouth glowed like a supernova, and he spewed fiery dragon breath.

Grayson blocked the fire with his shield. His ice floe started melting. Blood-Wing swooped closer. Grayson reinforced his shield, making it broader, thicker, colder. He stabbed his sword into the water. A bolt of ice cut across the waves and sprouted into an icy geyser that snatched the Sulfurian midair.

Blood-Wing twitched and jerked. He snaked his white-hot face around, melted his icy prison, and ascended higher. "You will not halt the coming of the next Great One, Frost-Keeper!" He blasted another jet of fire.

Grayson blocked with his shield. "Why do I get the feeling that this 'Great One' is not going to be so great for *me?*" He whipped a series of icy boomerangs from his sword.

The Sulfurian whirled and dodged every projectile. He dropped, spiraled, and within seconds, snatched Grayson's wrists. Blood-Wing's claws sank into Grayson's armor. The monster's mouth burned like an oven; smoke poured from his wings.

Grayson struggled. He put all his focus into staying iced up, keeping his sword securely frozen to his fist.

"The next Grand Sulfurian will bathe in the light of eternal flame!" Blood-Wing proclaimed. "And unending fire will swallow this human city!"

Grayson couldn't match the Sulfurian's strength. His Frost-Blade was stuck at an awkward angle. Instinctively, he turned his head to the side, inhaled deep, and then exhaled frosty air, right down Blood-Wing's throat.

Blood-Wing hacked and gagged. Frost crept across

his charcoal face. Steam poured from his mouth, and his claws instinctively went to his throat.

Grayson wrenched away, braced himself, and ice-surfed to safety.

Blood-Wing shook his wings and attempted to take off again. Grayson circled back and froze his opponent's legs. The Sulfurian crashed into the water; translucent wings splattered lake water. The Sulfurian's mouth glowed, and he aimed his face to melt the ice on his legs.

Before Blood-Wing could get airborne, Grayson surfed past and coated him in a layer of ice. "Just call me the human Zamboni machine. Do you guys have hockey in your evil fire dimension? Probably not, huh?"

A molten geyser shot up, freeing Blood-Wing's fiery head, but the rest of his body remained trapped. The Sulfurian screamed. Grayson's eardrums prickled. He circled back and glazed over the monster again, thickening his underwater trap, leaving Blood-Wing's head free.

"Pathetic human!" the Sulfurian shouted. "You will fail!" Fire poured from his mouth.

Grayson circled his enemy like an arctic shark. "Can't have you melting your way out, lava lips." He aimed his sword and froze Blood-Wing's neck upright, pointing the monster's fiery face at the sky. Then he slowed and leapt onto the glacier that trapped Blood-Wing.

Grayson crouched, put his fingertips to the ice and concentrated, making the icy prison as thick, deep, and cold as possible.

"Welcome to absolute zero, punk!" Grayson pointed to his Frost-Blade. "Now there's a reason I didn't just skewer you on this thing. I think we both know how that ends for you, flame brains."

Blood-Wing's face spouted white-hot geysers uselessly into the air. "I will evaporate your innards and burn your skin away!"

"I see you're in a chatty mood. Good." Grayson tickled Blood-Wing under the chin with the tip of his sword. "You see, this Frost-Key didn't come with instructions, and your people and I never really got a proper introduction. So, tell me: Who are you Sulfurians? Why are you here?"

The heat in the Sulfurian's face dimmed to an eerie orange glow. He scowled at the sky.

"Yeah, whatever, just take your time and collect your thoughts," Grayson said. "I'll just keep inching my Frost-Blade closer to your throat."

The pores of Blood-Wing's skin simmered like lava. His eyes winced with the bitterness of defeat. "We are many, human. And though I fear your weapon, you are still but one. The host has been chosen. Your city is doomed."

"The host of what?" Grayson asked. "Help me out here."

"The host will burn to cinders. Our glorious fires, fueled by his anger, will grant the Great One rebirth!" Blood-Wing laughed. Plumes of sulfur escaped his mouth. Lava dribbled down his chin and simmered against the ice.

Grayson concentrated a stream of cold around the Sulfurian's trap. "One stab and you're snowflakes melting in the summer sun, hot wings. So maybe start bargaining like your life depends on it. Which, keep in mind, it does."

Blood-Wing laughed harder. "You are feisty, but

easily distracted, Frost-Keeper 102. However, I do offer a bargain." Flames danced in the monster's eyes. "Spare me, or my subordinates will incinerate the small one before he hits ground."

Grayson's heart froze. He turned and spotted two more winged Sulfurians swooping toward the dock. Mason shouted as Blood-Wing's minions snatched him into the air.

Chapter 14

"**P**ut him down!" Grayson shouted.

Flames crackled in Blood-Wing's throat. "Humans are so predictable!"

Mason struggled. His tablet case plummeted into the lake as the winged Sulfurians carried him over the water, toward Grayson.

"Drop your weapon into the lake, boy," Blood-Wing demanded. "Or we kill this one."

"Don't do it!" Mason shouted. "They'll kill us both!"

Grayson's head pounded. Waves swelled and crashed. Sirens sounded in the distance. Fire engines and police cars converged past the shore, where the Sulfurians had set their blaze.

"You have ten seconds!" Blood-Wing snarled. "Drop your weapon, or my minions will spread this child's ashes across the surf!"

Mason locked eyes with Grayson. He shook his head.

Mason's right, he realized. *The Sulfurians blow up museums and vaporize people. They have no honor. If I drop my weapon, there's no way out.*

"Ten!" Blood-Wing snarled. "Nine!" Smoke

billowed from his mouth. "Eight!"

Waves swelled. Water lapped over Grayson's frosty ankles and froze into hypnotic crystals. Grayson tightened his fists. The air chilled.

"Seven!"

The winged drones cackled. Fire danced in their eyes.

"Six!"

Grayson swiped his sword and conducted a surge of arctic air. Blizzard force winds rushed around him. The two Sulfurians' wings snagged in the squall. Ice and snow coated their skin, and they dropped Mason.

A huge wave swelled, carried by his freak blizzard. Grayson manipulated the wave high into the air. Lake water curled and froze into a frozen slide that caught his brother. Mason slid thirty feet down to safety.

The winds died down. More water crashed around them. Mason struggled to stand on the icy mess Grayson had created. The top-heavy ice slide teetered backward.

"Stop them!" Blood-Wing snarled.

The Sulfurian soldiers righted themselves and shook the frost from their wings. They ignited like Roman candles and spat fireballs at Mason. Grayson was already ice-surfing to his brother at turbo speed. He scooped him out of the way.

Blood-Wing's drones dove after them, just as the enormous frozen slide capsized. Water and ice gushed up and pushed the creatures under.

"Hang on, Mace!" Grayson shouted. "We're getting out of here!"

"Stop them, you fools!" Blood-Wing's angry cries echoed.

Grayson swerved and made a beeline for the

distant Navy Pier Ferris Wheel. Mason wrapped his arms tight around his brother's torso. He shouted into Grayson's ear, "You're letting them get away!"

"I'm saving our lives!" Grayson shouted back. "Mace, these things are after me, not you. When I get you back to shore, go straight to Aunt Linda's condo and hide, okay?"

"What if they're waiting for me there?" Mason yelled. "What if they know our names? Grayson, I want to help you!"

Grayson increased his speed and shot further across the lake. He glanced back and saw clear skies. In the distance, a helicopter circled the pillar of black smoke by the marina. He spotted the mess of ice floating by the pier, but the flying Sulfurians themselves had vanished.

Grayson slowed. His ice board spread into a wide floating platform, and he nailed his sword into the floe to halt them. He held Mason steady as the new ice floe bobbed to rest.

"Mason!" Grayson's voice broke. "You almost died! Do you get that? This is serious."

Mason took a deep breath. He wiped frost off his glasses. "You might not like it, Gray, but the safest place for me right now is with *you*."

"I am *not* a superhero, okay? What happened back there was my fault. I never should have left you on shore alone."

"You can't be everywhere," Mason said. "And what happened was *their* fault—those stupid Sulfurians! You need to skewer them all before they hurt anyone else, and I want to help."

Grayson sighed. "You have, Mace. Just by believing me. What would really help now is knowing where to look for answers."

A cracking sounded. Mason pointed behind him. "How about that way?"

A series of icy arrows bobbed in the water. They pointed back toward the city. "More stupid arrows?" Grayson glared at the Frost-Blade. "Can't you tell me where to go in plain English?"

"They're pointing back downtown." Mason moved his finger along the skyline. "I hate to say it, but the Slynt Hotel is right behind those buildings."

"When we were at the Slynt, it told us to go north. When we got to the museum, it sent us to the beach. Now we're going back where we started? This stupid thing is broken!"

"Maybe what we're looking for is on the move?" Mason suggested.

"These arrows keep leading us to more Sulfurians," Grayson said. "If there's another fight at the hotel, I really don't want you with me."

"There's no safer place than with you," Mason insisted. "You know I'm right."

Grayson exhaled. "Okay. But we have to get back to shore without drawing attention. Every time I use my powers, those fiery freaks show up."

Mason rubbed his chin. "I've got an idea, but it won't be easy."

"Nothing about today has been easy." Grayson took a deep breath and slowly exhaled a cloud of frost. A pleasant chill swilled from the Frost-Key and cooled his blood. "Lay it on me, Mace. What's your idea?"

Chapter 15

Grayson's arms strained against the Chicago River. His ice canoe was stable, as was the double-edged ice paddle he had forged from the Frost-Key's handle. But the combined weight of two North brothers was slowing them down.

The River Walk in front of the Slynt Hotel was just beyond a group of kayaking tourists.

"This is taking forever." Grayson sighed. "If I was ice-surfing, we'd have been back twenty minutes ago."

"At least you're immune to the c-c-cold," Mason chattered. "My butt is f-f-freezing."

A kayaker glanced back. "Are you with our group?" he called out. "Where are your life jackets?"

"We're with an advanced group," Grayson said.

The man rolled his eyes and plowed forward. A tour boat passed by. Passengers started snapping pictures of Grayson and his brother.

"People are staring," Grayson said. "They can tell something's up with this boat."

"They don't know you have p-p-powers," Mason said. "They think this is a white c-c-canoe."

"Yeah, a *translucent* white canoe with a see-through paddle." Grayson waved sheepishly and strained forward.

The loudspeaker of the tour boat echoed. "Coming up on your right, check out the world-famous Slynt Hotel, the newest addition to our remodeled Chicago Riverwalk. Industrialist Alexander Slynt's vision for our newest Chicago icon took five years to build and incorporated cutting edge innovations in architectural design and renewable power, using rare Earth metals and advanced solar absorption panels. The entire hotel is energy self-sufficient, and even contributes to the power grid of surrounding infrastructure."

Grayson huffed and followed the wake of the tour boat. Once they were close to the Slynt, he made sure nobody was looking, then created a makeshift ice staircase, connecting their canoe to the concrete platform of the river walk. "Hurry, Mace!"

Mason carefully climbed the slick steps, and Grayson followed. He collapsed the double-edged paddle back into his Frost-Key. The icy steps and boat capsized and melted into the river.

As the brothers ascended the concrete steps to the Slynt lobby, soft cries echoed below.

Grayson peered around the edge of the steps. A girl in a black skirt and stylish boots huddled against the corner of the Riverwalk. Her face was buried in her hands, but Grayson instantly recognized the curtain of silky blond curls swaying over her hands.

"Um... Lucy?"

Lucy Slynt sniffled and wiped her eyes on her fists. She glanced up. Her eyes narrowed into daggers, but her voice came out broken and sad. "Mind your own business! It is not polite to stare!"

"Mason," he whispered, "could you give me a minute?"

Grayson cautiously approached Lucy. "Hey, I'm not staring. I just want to make sure everything is okay. I'm Grayson. We met this morning."

"I remember you! You were staring then, and you're staring now."

Grayson blushed. "Sorry."

"It's rude!"

"It's rude to like you?" Grayson sighed. "Look, I'm a cool guy if you just get to know me."

"You're just another crass American at this terrible hotel in this horrid city!"

"Hey!" Grayson snapped. "Sorry if you're homesick or whatever, but Chicago isn't a horrid city. There's lots of cool stuff and plenty of nice people."

"There are second-rate shops and second-rate museums and streets full of buffoons."

"I admit, I've run into a few unsavory characters today myself, but if you're seriously crying because you're a snob, I don't have time."

"I am crying because it is none of your business." She choked out another sob and grimaced. "Who would believe me, anyway?"

Grayson lowered his voice. "There's something bad going on, right? In the hotel."

Lucy's eyes widened.

"You saw something?"

Lucy shrugged. She shook her head in desperation. "Yes. I... I don't want to talk to *you* about it."

"Okay, Lucy. I'm sorry I called you a snob, but actually my brother and I were just—" Grayson glanced up, and suddenly noticed Mason was gone. He dashed back to the bottom of the staircase. He spotted his brother heading for the hotel lobby. "Hey,

Mason! Get back down here!"

Mason returned to the steps. "I thought you wanted to flirt with that girl," he said, a little too loudly. "Wouldn't be cool to have your little brother around for that."

"Heh." Grayson smiled sheepishly at Lucy Slynt, who finally cracked a smile in return. "Kids say the darndest things."

"I'm only two years younger than you." Mason shook his head as he descended the stairs.

Grayson tugged Mason down the last few steps and whispered to him. "I wanted you to hang back, not wander into danger. What if Sulfurians are up there?"

"First you want me to stay away," Mason said. "Now you won't let me wander twenty feet?"

"It's because I don't want anything bad to happen to you." He guided Mason back toward Lucy. "Lucy, this is my super-smart, super-awesome kid brother, Mason."

Lucy stood and wiped her eyes.

"Nice to meet you," Mason said. "Again."

"You have an overprotective brother, it seems." Lucy shook Mason's hand.

"You have no idea," Mason said.

"Lucy, this morning I saw a bunch of weird stuff— in the hotel—and nobody believed me," Grayson said. "Nobody except Mason. So, if you saw something weird, we want to know all about it."

Lucy sighed. "It's too crazy."

Mason and Grayson exchanged glances. "If you can top today's trend of one crazy thing after the next," Grayson said, "then I will eat this ice cream scooper." He held up the Frost-Key and found it was now in flashlight form. "Er... flashlight."

Lucy took a close look at the flashlight. Her eyes grew wide. She reached for it, and Grayson instinctively pulled his hand back.

She looked up. "May I see it? For just a moment?"

Grayson reluctantly handed the flashlight to her.

Lucy turned it over and studied it. "*Mon Dieu!*" she exclaimed. "Where did you find this?"

"Let's say it was a gift." Grayson snatched the flashlight back. "Why? Have you seen it before today?"

"No," Lucy said. "But strange metal just like this is in the walls of the hotel. In the subbasement. I saw plans. Pictures and schematics for four pillars."

"Where did you see this?"

Lucy scowled. "On *her* tablet." She hit *her* with special bitterness. "Joanna Crisp."

"Your dad's fiancée?" Mason asked. "The blind lady?"

"She's *not* a lady," Lucy said. "She is some kind of—"

"Monster," Grayson finished.

Lucy's jaw dropped. She nodded.

Grayson recalled the creepy feeling he'd had at Something Suite earlier when Joanna stared right through him, just before he had been attacked. *Did she know I have the Frost-Key?* he wondered.

Lucy continued, "Joanna caught me looking at her files. She cornered me and showed me her palm. Her hand glowed. And soon, all I could see was an abyss of flames. At first, I was mesmerized. I only wanted to surrender. To forget what I saw. But then, I thought about Joanna, with my father, the two of them married. I couldn't stand it. I fought for control. I broke free and tried to escape. But her security guards stopped me. They were rough, angry."

"Were they wearing sunglasses indoors?" Grayson asked.

"Some of them, yes!" Lucy said. "Joanna tried to show me the swirling fire again, but it wasn't working. She started screaming. Then my father showed up." Fresh tears slid down Lucy's cheeks. "I was certain he would protect me."

"Lucy," Grayson said. "Is your dad okay?"

"I don't know. He shouted at me. Told me I was a spoiled, selfish child, and that I was a burden on him and Joanna. That he wished he didn't have to deal with me. He was shaking with anger. His face was red, like a volcano."

"Interesting comparison," Mason whispered.

Lucy sobbed. "Grayson, you have to understand. My father didn't get to be who he is by having meltdowns and screaming at people. I have never seen him that way before. It was like he was..."

"A different person," Mason said.

Grayson put his hand on Lucy's shoulder. "Lucy, I hate to even ask, but... how well do you know your father?"

"My mother was his third wife. I see him a few times a year," she admitted. "He is very busy, but he calls every day. He *does* love me. He insisted that I fly in for his engagement party. He meant it as a surprise for Joanna, but since I arrived, they've both been distant and strange."

Mason tugged at Grayson's shirt and whispered— once again a little too loudly, "Do you think Slynt is a Sulfurian?"

"Sulfurian?" Lucy glanced between the two brothers.

"Mason, you need to work on volume control," Grayson said. "Would you believe us if we said fire monsters are invading Chicago?"

Lucy scoffed. "You think my father is a monster?"

"These creatures, the Sulfurians, wear human skin," Mason explained.

"My father is a good man," Lucy insisted. "People act like he is a monster because he is wealthy, but he is a hardworking, decent person. It's *her*! Joanna is the monster."

"I agree," Grayson said. "Your dad has normal human eyes. Sulfurians wear shades to hide their fiery innards, like that security guy Cortez and those goons from the lobby."

"Joanna has human eyes too, though," Mason noted.

"But she's blind," Grayson said. "Seems like a pretty good cover. And I swear, I felt her staring right at me this morning. Plus that hypnotic fire trick you described, Lucy. Someone's been altering perceptions, blanking people's memories around the hotel and at the museum. Aunt Linda didn't even remember the accident this morning."

"That flash of light on the security footage!" Mason said. "What if that was some kind of subliminal message, and it only made us *think* we saw something that didn't happen?"

Grayson groaned. "Fireballs, lava claws, incineration breath, flight, and apparently we can officially add mind control to the list of a zillion reasons why Sulfurians are the worst things ever! What do you know about Joanna Crisp, Lucy? How did your dad meet her in the first place?"

"Joanna oversaw construction and development of the Slynt Hotel," Lucy explained. "She used this same shimmering copper-colored metal." She pointed to the flashlight. "So tell me, Grayson North, what exactly is this flashlight made of?"

"From what I hear: adaptanium."

"What is adaptanium?"

"It's metal that... well here, let me show you." Grayson focused, and a bouquet of frosty ice roses swirled onto the end of the flashlight.

Lucy covered her mouth in surprise.

Cold air puffed from Grayson's lips. "Told you I was a cool guy!"

Chapter 16

Lucy Slynt marveled as Grayson sculpted ice hearts, flowers, and figurines atop the lens of his adaptanium flashlight.

Eventually, Mason grabbed Grayson's wrist to stop him. "Gray! You're making a scene."

An architectural tour boat drifted by. Passengers were capturing photos and video of Grayson's tricks.

"Sleight of hand illusions, people! Nothing fancy!" Grayson shouted. "Check out a book on magic at the library. You can do it, too!" Grayson smiled at Lucy. "Maybe we should head someplace quieter and talk. If the hotel is really built from the same metal as my Frost-Key, that could be seriously dangerous."

"I don't think the Frost-Key wants us to go back to the hotel," Mason said.

"What? I thought we agreed the arrow was pointing..." Grayson glanced down. Three new frozen arrows pointed downriver, then curved north, back in the direction of the history museum. "What? It wants us to go back to the museum? The beach? I'm so lost."

Lucy examined the frosty arrows. "You've been following these?"

"All freakin' day!"

Mason pulled out his phone and showed Lucy a satellite view of the city. "Earlier, the key directed us from the hotel in this direction. Then from the museum, kinda toward shore, then from the water back this way..." Mason placed markers on each spot where an arrow had appeared.

"You're being directed somewhere between the hotel, the museum, and the lake," Lucy explained. "Here." She tapped Mason's phone and the map zoomed in on North Michigan Avenue. "This is the region where all the paths intersect."

"There's nothing there but Michigan Avenue shopping and the Water Tower Place Mall," Grayson said.

Mason's eyes lit up. "That's it! The Water Tower!"

"Why would a mystic relic want us to go shopping?" Grayson asked. He held the flashlight to his face and shouted. "We have bigger priorities, Frost-Key!"

"Not the mall," Mason said. "The *actual* stone Chicago Water Tower that the mall is named after."

"Why would it want us to go there?" Grayson asked.

Mason ran a quick search on his phone. "Here's a fun fact: The Water Tower is the *only* landmark still standing since the Great Chicago Fire!"

Grayson smiled. "Who wants to go sightseeing?"

The three of them headed up the steps toward the lobby entrance. "It's not far," Grayson said. "We can probably walk. I'd ice-surf us upriver, but I'm afraid a horde of Sulfurians might try to fry us."

"Don't be absurd." Lucy brushed her hair behind her ears. "I have a driver." She marched toward the hotel valet.

Grayson gripped his brother's arm. "She has a

driver! Mason, I don't want to jump to any conclusions, but I think that's your future sister-in-law."

"Grayson!" came a familiar shout.

Their brother Jason approached. His arms were stained with chocolate. His eyes were narrowed with irritation. "I thought I saw you out here. Aunt Linda told you guys to go straight home and stay there."

"She did," Grayson said. "But the thing is—wait a minute. You remember what happened this morning? Sulfurians didn't wipe your mind?"

"I remember you're all messed up in the head, telling stories about freezer men and making a scene in the lobby, yes! I don't want you running around with our little brother when—"

"Jason, hang on! This is important—"

"Do you have any idea how much Aunt Linda put herself out on the line for you today? How hard I had to work to clean up your mess!"

"Hang on. Why didn't Aunt Linda remember—"

"Listen to me!" Jason shouted.

"Jason!" Mason spoke up. "Please! We have to show you something."

Jason glared between his two brothers. "What?" Jason's scowl landed on Grayson.

"Why do you only look at *me* that way?" Grayson asked.

Jason shook his head. "What are you talking about?"

"Like you *hate* me."

"I hate the way you've been behaving."

"Gray!" Mason squeezed Grayson's fingers around the flashlight. "Go ahead. Show him!"

Grayson glanced around. The valets were occupied. Lucy was watching from the entranceway. Nobody in sight was wearing shades.

Mason's right, he thought. *Once Jason sees my powers, he'll lighten up. He'll help us.*

Grayson tried his hardest to focus. But his hand trembled. His head surged with anger. His knees buckled. Nothing happened. The Frost-Blade refused to appear.

Jason's glare intensified.

The way Jason's looking at me right now, Grayson realized. *That's how he looks at Dad.*

"Come on, Gray!" Mason whispered. "Do it!"

"It's..." Grayson shook his head. Tears welled. "Forget it."

"Take our brother home," Jason snapped. "Aunt Linda and I have so much to do for Slynt's party tonight. Thanks to you, we're behind on everything."

Grayson shook with anger. "It's all about you, Jason. I get it."

"I don't have time for this. Starting tomorrow, you need to step up, Gray." Jason stormed back into the hotel.

"Grayson? Mason? Are you ready?" A chrome limousine pulled into the hotel's circular drive and stopped in front of Lucy.

"That is the coolest car I've ever seen." Grayson stewed. "And I'm too mad to be impressed."

"Why didn't your powers work?" Mason whispered as they headed toward the limo.

"I don't know," Grayson said. "But right now, this whole Frost-Keeper thing feels like a joke at my expense. If I don't get answers soon, I really will go crazy."

Chapter 17

Grayson sank into the L-shaped leather seat of the Slynt limo. Complimentary sparkling water lined an ice-filled trough that glowed in soft blue light. Grayson imagined this was what prom must be like, minus the fire monsters.

"This is weird," Mason said, checking his smart phone. "You'd think with all the crazy stuff going on in the city today there'd be something—anything—about it in the news. Two major fires downtown, tons of potential witnesses for both of Grayson's battles... There's nothing on social media except this one article."

"'Museum Fire Ruled an Accident!'" Grayson shouted. "What the heck! *Everyone* saw Scarlett Fury tossing fireballs!"

"It's that swirling fire," Lucy said. "They're controlling people."

"Wait a minute." Mason squinted at his phone. "'Unprecedented El Niño weather patterns cause ice formations in July.' Well, that makes sense." He glanced up and smiled.

"Uh, Mace?" Grayson asked. "I made those ice formations."

Mason stared blankly. "That doesn't make much sense."

Grayson pointed to his flashlight. "It doesn't, but it's happening."

"We just got carried away." Mason shrugged. "We should head home and forget about all this."

Grayson snatched his brother's phone. In the sidebar of an online article, a rotating fiery pattern accompanied a picture of Grayson's capsized ice ramp. "Whoa!" Grayson pocketed his brother's phone. "Mason, think! There's no ice in summertime on the Great Lakes! Frost-Key. Sulfurians." He snapped his fingers in front of his brother's eyes.

Mason squinted and rubbed his forehead. "Right! Right! No wonder everyone is acting so weird. The Sulfurians must have plants in the media. Those hypnotic gifs must be packed with subliminal advertising or something."

"Joanna used the same swirling fire on me," Lucy said. "But I resisted it."

"Okay," Grayson said. "Everybody, stop checking your phones."

The limo pulled alongside the Jane M. Byrne Plaza. The driver opened the door. "Shall I circle for you, Ms. Slynt?"

The three of them climbed out, and Lucy handed the driver a fifty dollar bill. "No, *merci*. And please say nothing of my whereabouts to my father. I will text when we are ready for pickup."

The driver smiled. "I can't promise that, Ms. Slynt, but I'll be ready anytime." The driver tipped his hat, got back inside, and pulled away.

All along Michigan Avenue, shoppers and tourists were still out, but in noticeably fewer numbers. "Slow shopping day," Grayson observed.

The white stone Chicago Water Tower rose three stories, surrounded by spires and castle ramparts. It looked like a medieval watchtower, displaced in time among modern skyscrapers.

Mason approached a bronze plaque. "The Water Tower isn't the only Chicago building to survive the fire, I guess, but it's the most famous one. Says here it was built in 1869. It was used to store and pump water, which would help fight fires. Now it's the Chicago Tourism Office."

Grayson smiled at Lucy. "My brother reads plaques for me."

Lucy rolled her eyes.

A chill crawled over Grayson's fingers. He glanced down. His flashlight had become a key once more. "We're in the right place. Come on."

Grayson led them through the main door into the white waiting room, or what his mom would call "the antechamber." A smiling young woman sat behind a counter flanked by city brochures and pamphlets.

"Good afternoon! Welcome to the Chicago Water Tower!" the woman exclaimed. "Would you like to schedule a tour? Do you have any questions about the city?"

Grayson laughed. "Oh boy, do I have questions! Know anything about Sulfurian fire monsters, Frost-Keepers, or ancient mystical ice-weaponry?"

The woman winced. "Can't say that I do."

"Figures." Grayson shrugged. "We came to the wrong place, then. Have a good one!"

Lucy and Mason followed Grayson out. The door

slammed behind them.

Lucy huffed. "Do you know what it means to be subtle, Grayson North?"

"Trust me," Grayson said.

"Why did we come here if we're not going to explore inside?" Lucy asked.

Grayson concentrated. "Sometimes there's more than one inside to something. Something else is here. I can feel it."

"Feel it how?" Lucy asked.

"Tough to explain. Like coolant in my blood. Freezer sense." He held his key in front of him. Icicles dripped from the tip. A drop of ice splattered on the ground and froze into an arrow that curved around the Water Tower. Grayson smiled. "This way!"

Cold air swirled from Grayson's breath as he raced around the building. "There!"

Centered in white brick was the same coppery-silver keyhole that had appeared on the walk-in freezer. Grayson glanced around. He scanned the sky for airborne Sulfurians. Then he approached the keyhole and unlocked it.

White bricks groaned, folded, and slid inside the wall. A blue glow shone outward. Frosty air steamed into the hot afternoon. "Bundle up, kids," Grayson said. "Looks like it's cold in there."

Grayson led Lucy and Mason into the chilly interior. The inside was completely hollow. The walls dripped with gigantic icicles. In the center of the tower, spiral steps—made entirely of ice—coiled up to a pitch black opening in the ceiling.

"How is this possible?" Mason marveled.

The wall grated behind them. They turned to discover that the exit had frozen back over, sealing them inside.

Lucy shivered. "We're trapped!"

"It's okay," Grayson assured them. "This place feels safe. Stick with me." Grayson led them to the winding staircase. "No bannister? Are you kidding me?" From his Frost-Key, Grayson fired a strip of ice that crawled up the edges of the staircase forming a safety handle. "Still be careful," he smiled at Lucy. "It's slippery."

She rolled her eyes, then slipped and caught herself on the rungs of Grayson's bannister. Before Grayson could open his mouth, she said, "I can manage," and carefully started to follow him up the steps.

Cool mist rolled down the steps. Their footfalls echoed up the spire. Mason and Lucy took their time, carefully maneuvering the slick staircase, but Grayson's feet had a sixth sense for balance. By the time he was halfway up, he had let go of the bannister.

At the top step, three stories up, Grayson found an adaptanium ladder that led up a shadowy stone tube. His key thickened into a flashlight, and he lit his way into the dark open area.

Grayson emerged in an enormous dome. He shone his flashlight in a circle. Tables, maps, tools, weapons, drawings, paintings, and other artifacts in glass cases surrounded him. The dome above their heads was glass, but for some reason it was night outside. White flurries swirled in the sky, like a beautiful winter snowstorm.

Slowly, the entire dome glowed with blue light.

Eerie calmness swept over Grayson. He felt his flashlight shift back into a key. *Something is really right about this snow globe room,* he realized. *For the first time in months—maybe years—it feels like I'm home.*

Lucy pulled herself up into the wintery dome. Her eyes widened with astonishment. *"Qu'est-ce que c'est! Oh, mon Dieu!"*

Grayson helped her and Mason onto the landing. His brother marveled at the winter skylight. "We're in another dimension!" he proclaimed. "A pocket dimension, like where you found the other Frost-Keeper, Victor Drake, in the freezer!"

Grayson held up his key. "This metal changes form when you're not looking. It opens pocket spaces that shouldn't fit inside things. Victor must have reinforced the Water Tower with adaptanium to keep everything safe."

Lucy crossed to a case containing an old-fashioned dress uniform, a long, rubbery jacket, boots, a helmet, and a fireman's ax. Soft lights illuminated the case as she approached. She read the name tag. "'Victor Drake.' He gave you this key?"

Grayson nodded. "This was his base of operations." Relief washed over him. "This is where the Frost-Key has been trying to take us all day! Everybody look around. I'm not totally sure what we're searching for, but I think we'll know it when we see it."

A historical map of Chicago adorned one wall, dated 1909. "I guess since the tower survived the fire, and Victor was a firefighter, the tower was his best option for a headquarters."

Lucy gasped at a hand-drawn chart. "These are the monsters?" Sketches of different Sulfurians were arranged in a pyramid. In black ink, the chart header read *Sulfurian Caste System.*

Grayson scanned the hierarchy of creatures. He squinted to read the curvy scripted notes. "'Sulfurian drones are used mostly for reconnaissance and have low-grade pyro-kinetic attributes.' Those are the bozos I fought in the lobby."

The drawing of the warrior class Sulfurians showed longer necks, bigger, sharper claws, and tall plumes of flames around their hands. "'Warrior elite.' That's my lady friend, Scarlett Fury!" Grayson pointed at a bat-winged drawing. "'Sulfurian waifs!' That's Blood-Wing and his beach buddies!"

Another drawing showed a tall, lanky Sulfurian with a smaller head and beadier eyes. It held a swirling fiery pattern on the claws of one hand. "'Sulfurian mages,'" Grayson read, "'manipulate the mind with hypnotic fire.'"

Lucy's eyes narrowed. "Joanna."

"And apparently hypno-fire works on security footage *and* online," Grayson said. "Whatever they're planning, they're desperate to keep a low profile, and I gotta say, they're pretty good at fooling the whole city."

"My father!" Lucy's voice trembled. "Grayson, we have to bring him here, where he'll be safe."

"Hang on, Lucy," Grayson said. "I'll do whatever I can, but we need a plan first." Grayson studied the top of the Sulfurian caste chart. The upper slot on the pyramid showed a circular opening—a portal projecting two furious eyes, with long licks of flame forming a beard that spilled downward.

Lucy read the notes. "'The Grand Sulfurian has never set foot in the human realm but is believed to be unstoppable.'"

Grayson flashed back to the blazing portal that

Scarlett Fury opened in the Red Line tunnel. "Scarlett's boss."

"You guys!" Mason hunched over an old-fashioned desk against the far side of the dome. He held up a huge leatherbound book. "Check this out!"

Grayson crossed the room. The book was five inches thick and wider than his brother's shoulders. The title had been stitched into the binding with silvery threads. "'Chronicles of the 101st Frost-Keeper, Sworn Protector of Humanity,'" he read. "Finally! Answers!"

Chapter 18

Grayson and Lucy read over Mason's shoulder as he pored over Victor Drake's journal.

"The good news is Victor Drake's records are pretty organized," Mason said. "There's a lot here about the Frost-Keeper and his powers. There's a huge section about Sulfurians, too, and memoirs about Victor's adventures."

"What's the bad news?" Grayson asked.

"This is a really long, really old book." Mason delicately turned frayed, yellowed pages. "Looks like some sections are missing, too. In the back here, Victor started to record details about the other one hundred Frost-Keepers, but I guess he died before he could finish it."

"He didn't die," Grayson said. "He just went into a pocket dimension and entered cryogenesis until I came along. And, uh... *then* he died."

Mason flipped to the table of contents. "There's a section on cryogenesis, too." Mason cleaned his glasses on his shirt. "This is going to take forever to sort through."

"But you love books, Mace!" Grayson patted his

brother's back. "I know you can make sense of this one."

Mason frowned. "I'm not used to sorting through ancient texts with a city in peril."

"Yeah, well I'm only thirteen, and I'm not used to fighting fire monsters with an ice sword," Grayson said. "Whoever said life was fair?"

"Start with one topic at a time," Lucy suggested. "What do these Sulfurians want? Why are they here?"

Mason skimmed the table of contents and opened to a page titled *The Menace of the Sulfurian Empire*. His eyes darted down the page. He was reading faster than Grayson could think.

"The Sulfurians aren't demons *or* aliens," Mason said. "According to this, they're 'extra-dimensional elementals.' They come from a realm too hot for life to develop. But their body chemistry lets them survive."

"That doesn't make sense," Grayson said. "If life can't develop in their dimension, why do they exist?"

Mason kept reading. "Millennia ago, Sulfurians were 'born of human hatred,' and that's the only way they can reproduce. Once a century, when the current Grand Sulfurian's life cycle is close to complete, they return to Earth to make a new leader by 'incubating a germ in the recesses of human rage.'"

"What kind of germ?" Grayson asked. "Like a disease?"

"Germinate," Lucy said. "A seed that needs to grow."

"Sounds like it," Mason said. "It's a special royal egg or something that goes in a person. The germ takes over that person's mind and body. It 'burns the human away in fires of rage,' and replaces them."

Lucy gasped. "My father!"

A grim silence filled the wintery dome. Finally, Grayson said, "Could the germ be inside Lucy's dad?"

"It makes sense," Mason said. "If I was an evil Sulfurian choosing a host for my new leader, I'd take over the life of a rich and powerful person like Mr. Slynt."

"Plus, with Joanna the Fire Mage as his fiancée, they've got him on a short leash, don't they?" Grayson sighed.

"Please, Grayson," Lucy said. "We have to save him."

Grayson's stomach sank. *If the Sulfurian germ burns people's essence away, and the only way to stop a Sulfurian is with my Frost-Blade, then the only way to save Lucy's dad might be…*

Grayson buried the thought. "We *will* save him, Lucy. Mason, keep reading, okay? I want you to look for something, anything that says how to remove that germ, safely."

"Okay," Mason said.

"Meanwhile, I need a favor from you too, Lucy."

"Anything," she said. "Anything to help my father."

Grayson smiled. "Can I borrow some money?"

Chapter 19

Mason remained in the wintery dome, studying the Frost-Keeper's journal, while Grayson and Lucy descended the spiral staircase. Grayson leapt onto the bannister and slid all the way down, backwards.

"Careful!" Lucy shouted.

"It's okay!" Grayson nimbly hopped to the frozen floor. "I'm a professional!"

Lucy awkwardly descended one slick step after the next.

"To be honest, even before I got this Frost-Keeper gig, I was pretty good at sliding down bannisters. I only got seriously injured six times."

Lucy slipped on the final step and Grayson caught her.

He smiled. "Careful."

She jerked away and tossed her hair behind her shoulders.

Grayson approached the wall, and the exit slid open all on its own. "Nice! Automatic door. Wouldn't want Mace to get trapped in there." He poked his head outside to make sure nobody was watching, then signaled for Lucy to follow. The white brick ground shut behind them.

"You care about your brother," Lucy said.

"Yes, I do." Grayson led the way toward the Water Tower Place Mall. The afternoon sun hung low. The streets were even more vacant. Traffic was light. Too light.

"How about you?" Grayson asked. "Any brothers or sisters?"

"I have two sisters and one brother. All much older. All in different countries. I do not know any of them well."

"Maybe you should get to know them better."

"Why?" Lucy asked.

"Because my little brother is fast becoming my favorite person in the world. If anything ever happened to him, I'd never forgive myself. I can't imagine not having him in my life."

They waited to cross Michigan Avenue. "What about your older brother?" Lucy asked.

"Jason's a jerk. He'll be happy once he's at college and doesn't have to worry about us anymore. He thinks our parents are getting divorced and just wants to start his own life."

The walk sign illuminated, and they crossed toward the mall. "I understand how he feels," Lucy said.

"You love your dad, right?" Grayson asked.

"Of course! He works hard to provide his children with the very best. But still, my mother resents him."

"So think of it this way," Grayson said. "Your brother and sisters must be worth knowing, because they're at least a little bit like you and your dad, right?"

"I suppose."

"Who knows, maybe when this whole thing is over,

and we save your dad, he'll be so grateful that he'll give things with you and your mom another chance. Maybe they'll get back together."

Lucy glared. "Why would you say that?"

Grayson stared back. "Why not?"

"Because." She shook her head. "That's never going to happen."

"You never know. My parents have had rough times too, but people change. Jason is so sure they're getting divorced, but he's wrong."

Lucy's eyes carefully searched Grayson's. "Why do you think he's wrong?"

"My dad told me not to worry while we were away this summer. He promised he would step up, do the right thing, and make everything better."

Lucy's eyes softened. "Oh."

"So yeah." Grayson shrugged. "No big deal, right? Bad times happen, and then good times happen. Your parents could end up together again too."

They pushed through the revolving glass doors. Only a handful of shoppers lingered by the lobby escalators. Levels of ornate fountains led up the steps to the main spire of the Water Tower Mall. Drip-drops spouted up and down decorative tiered pools. But the stairs and escalators were completely empty.

"Okay this is creepy," Grayson observed. "It's a heat wave. This is an air-conditioned mall. It's Saturday. Where are all the shoppers and tourists?"

A familiar *prick-prock* sounded: high heels! Hair bristled on Grayson's neck. "Hide!"

He pulled Lucy toward the escalators. They crouched behind the menu stand for an Asian Fusion restaurant. A cashier stared at them in confusion.

Grayson put his finger over his lips and winked at the cashier. "Um. It's a game we're playing. Don't give us away, please."

The cashier rolled her eyes then went back to cleaning the counter.

The high heel echoes continued, and Scarlett Fury—in all her bright red glory—marched in view from the department store on the left. Her skin glowed around the edges of her black shades. Her red curls swirled like flame.

"She's the Sulfurian who's been hunting me," Grayson whispered to Lucy. "If she spots me, run!"

Lucy nodded.

Please don't find us, please don't find us, Grayson thought. The last thing he needed was another fight at another Chicago landmark.

"Hotstreak!" Scarlett pointed at the ground in front of her. "Get over here!" A scarecrow thin man in gym shoes, khakis and a Hawaiian shirt wandered into view. Large reflective shades covered his pimpled face. "How are the upstairs floors?"

"Nearly clear," he rasped. "Shall we close the businesses? Send the workers away?"

"It doesn't matter," Scarlett said. "The Grand Sulfurian does not require a complete evacuation, just general disinterest. Blood-Wing's scouts just want to clear the Loop and Magnificent Mile. Once the population is nice and dormant, we begin purification rituals."

"Excuse me," the Asian Fusion cashier called out. "Can I help you people?"

Scarlett Fury huffed and gestured toward the girl. "Shut her up."

Hotstreak held out his hand and a bright orange fireball swirled in the air. The fiery pattern caught Grayson's eyes, and he found himself staring into it. Suddenly, Lucy covered his vision. She whispered.

"Look away! He's a mage!"

"You will ignore us and all our activity," came the crackling voice of the Sulfurian. "After your shift is over, you will return home and stay indoors."

The worker's face went blank, and she began to obliviously clean the counter once more.

Scarlett Fury glared through the revolving glass doors. Suddenly strange, orange lights were drifting down the sidewalk. Hypno-fire floated in the air. "The streets will be empty soon. You mages have done well. Let's see if they require assistance outside. Stay alert for that pathetic little Frost-Keeper. He's bound to turn up soon."

Scarlett's heels echoed as they pushed their way out the revolving doors. Outside, Hotstreak summoned another ball of hypno-fire. He tossed it into the air, and it floated away like a ghost. The two Sulfurians headed down Michigan Avenue, out of view.

Grayson and Lucy exhaled. "Whatever they're planning, they must want as few witnesses as possible," Grayson said. "They're clearing the streets, mesmerizing people to stay indoors."

"When Mason saw the online image, he said the same thing," Lucy said. "We should go home."

"We better hurry." Grayson led Lucy up the escalator. Blobs of fountain water spouted between decorative plants. Pop music drifted from speakers.

"Grayson," Lucy asked. "Why are you doing this?"

"Doing what? Helping you?"

"Fighting monsters. You're putting yourself in danger."

"It's my first day as the 102nd Frost-Keeper, Lucy. So aside from the fact that my Frost-Blade looks like the only thing that can stop those jokers, I just want to do a good job."

Lucy smiled. "Well, thank you."

"You're welcome."

Grayson and Lucy took the glass elevator up. Lucy looked down through the transparent floor as the bottom of the tower lowered away. She gazed at each level of shops and decorations.

"Have you been here before?"

She shook her head.

"Ever since I started my job with Aunt Linda a few months ago, I've come here a few times a week. I've been saving my paychecks to get cool stuff for my room back home. Maybe after we save the world, we can hang out here some time?"

Lucy rolled her eyes. "I am not especially interested in making a date right now, Grayson."

"What can I say? I'm a multitasker." The elevator stopped at floor eight. Grayson led Lucy to a stylish shop with a neon sign that read *Gadgets N' Stuff.*

Rows of sleek, trendy merchandise lined the shelves: black lights, industrial blenders, fitness trackers, stainless-steel nose hair trimmers, and massage chairs—but Grayson headed right for a glass case by the register. He pointed out a paperclip-sized device.

"This is a top of the line receiver that syncs with your smartphone. It has military grade components, ultra-strong reception, and tucks right into your ear. My phone still had reception in the pocket dimension of the tower, so that means with this earpiece in place, you and Mason can stay behind where it's safe and feed me information about the Sulfurians from Victor's journal."

Lucy nodded. "Good idea!"

"Uh… the only problem is," Grayson said, "it's a tad

pricy."

A salesman in a Gadgets N' Stuff polo appeared behind the counter. "There's no other product like it on the market," he said. "Mountain climbers, deep sea divers, and whitewater rafters all use it to stay informed and in touch. But your friend is right. That little beauty carries a $2,999.99 price tag."

Lucy didn't even blink at the price. "We'll take three."

The salesman continued. "It does work with any smartphone or plan, and it's easy to set up. Virtually indestructible. Comes with GPS tracking in case of theft..." He raised an eyebrow. "Did you just say you want *three*? Three of *these*?"

Lucy produced a platinum credit card imprinted with a shimmering gold Slynt logo and placed it on the counter, next to her passport.

The salesman raised an eyebrow.

"Call the verification number on back. They will approve this purchase," Lucy instructed.

The salesman hesitantly picked up the card and Lucy's passport and headed to the phone behind the counter.

"Okay, that was pretty cool, Lucy, but we really just need *one* earpiece for me," Grayson said.

"Mason needs one, and so do I," she insisted. "Three. And whatever else these should come with, chargers, extra batteries, et cetera."

"That's ridiculously generous," Grayson said. "But seriously. You guys can just put Mason's phone on speaker."

"I am going back to the hotel with you, and I want to be able to hear everything."

"You can't go back to the hotel," Grayson said. "It's too dangerous."

"I am not your little brother, Grayson North. You cannot tell me what to do. I know my father's staff, and I know more about the hotel, plus I am the one who saw the Sulfurians' architectural plans."

The salesperson cleared his throat. "Wow, you kids are having an imaginative day." He had gathered a pile of accessories next to the boxed devices. "But apparently, Ms. Slynt is *indeed* authorized to use this card. So, shall I ring this up?"

Grayson shrugged. "Charge away. Her dad can afford it."

About $10,000 later, they hurried back to the glass elevator with a shopping bag full of cutting-edge tech. "We should stop at the electronics store outside as well," Lucy said. "Mason may have to cross reference information online. But he'll have to stay away from social media and the news."

"Since you're in such a giving mood, Mace did kinda lose his tablet in the lake." Grayson hit the button, and the elevator glided down. "Remind me to speak up next time someone acts like money doesn't solve problems."

Lucy's eyes grew wide. Her jaw dropped.

"What?" Grayson started to turn, but Lucy grabbed his shirt collar. She yanked him close and pressed her lips against his.

Grayson's heart fluttered. He closed his eyes and wrapped his arms around Lucy. Her hands glided to his neck and pulled him closer. Her fingernails dug into his neck. It was getting uncomfortable.

"Uh-Luschy—thish ish a little rough-mmph!"

Lucy pressed their faces together tighter, harder. Grayson's eyes jerked open and he spotted the Sulfurian's Hawaiian shirt—in the reflection of the elevator—stalking past the glass doors.

They descended further down. Lucy shoved Grayson away and wiped her lips once the Sulfurian was out of view. She shivered. "That was like kissing a freezer!"

"Oh, come on! It couldn't have been that bad." Grayson's breath puffed an icy cloud. "Uh... sorry." They hurried toward the exit. "Watch out for fire mages. Don't look at any glowing lights," Grayson warned her.

"They're after you, not me," she said. "You're the one who must be careful."

Outside, Lucy headed to the electronics store next to Water Tower Place. Grayson cautiously made his way back to the tower. He crossed the street, then averted his eyes when a swirling light rounded the corner.

Grayson glanced around to make sure nobody was watching. Then he aimed his Frost-Key and fired a quick blast of cool air. The spiraling flame faded into sparks and vanished. *Good to know the Frost-Key can snuff out these stupid hypno-flames.*

He rendezvoused with Mason at the top of the wintery dome, unpacked the Gadgets N' Stuff bag, and showed Mason the earpieces. "Lucy bought us some awesome tech so we can all stay in touch, buddy. She's even getting you a computer for online research. We figured this place is a little retro and could use some updating. I love rich people!"

"Great," Mason said. "Only where do we plug in?" Mason looked around. "This place is over one hundred years old."

Like magic, a silvery-copper plate—with three-pronged holes—formed on the table. Grayson grinned. "An outlet! The Frost-Keeper's adaptanium lair provides!"

Mason studied the mysterious metal rectangle. "I have got to figure out how this stuff works."

"Hey, guess what!" Grayson boasted. "She kissed me, Mace! Only to help us hide from a Sulfurian, and she seemed pretty disgusted by the whole thing, but I'd call that progress. Wouldn't you?"

"I'd call *this* progress." Mason pointed to a sketch in Victor Drake's journal. A cross-section of a human head showed a man's brain, and a fiery ember just behind the eyes. "That's the germ. Look." He flipped the page. "Victor Drake left instructions about how to kill the germ without injuring the host, but you have to do it before it develops too much."

"Awesome!" Grayson said. "Piece of cake!"

Mason glared. "No, Gray. Not a piece of cake. It's basically brain surgery, only with ice. If you screw up or take too long…"

Grayson's heart sank. "Great. I have to perform a life-threatening operation on Lucy's dad. No pressure, right?"

Chapter 20

Lucy texted Grayson to meet at the tower's hidden entrance. She arrived bearing a state of the art all-in-one computer, a wireless router, and two tablets that were top of the line.

They worked together to set up the equipment in the dome, transforming the sanctuary from the turn of the twentieth century into a hybrid of antiques and modern tech. Adaptanium outlets appeared like magic in every spot where they needed to set up equipment.

Grayson and Lucy tested their earpieces as they descended the icy staircase once more. Mason counted off as they exited into the sunny Chicago afternoon. "Testing! One, two, three! Can you guys still hear me?"

"Loud and clear," Grayson said.

"That must mean the pocket dimension isn't exactly a separate universe," Mason said. "Just extra folded-up space in our world that this weird metal keeps stable."

Michigan Avenue looked like an eerie ghost town. Only a few buses and cabs appeared in service.

Grayson averted his eyes when he noticed hypno-fire swirling atop streetlights.

"I should blast some of these hypno-orbs." He aimed the Frost-Key at the tips of nearby lamp posts and snuffed out the churning balls of flame.

"Don't draw attention," Lucy warned. "My chauffeur will arrive in five minutes." Lucy glanced down the street. "Those Sulfurians could still be close."

"I think they did their part clearing downtown," Grayson said. "But feel free to kiss me again, just to be safe."

Lucy scowled.

"It wasn't *that* bad!" He froze away another ball of hypno-fire.

Lucy crossed her arms. "It was like kissing a dead penguin."

"Ouch!" Grayson held a hand over his heart. "Come on, who wouldn't want to kiss something cold in the middle of a heat wave?" He snuffed another fireball.

Lucy's eyes sharpened; her scowl deepened.

"Gah! You have a *look*!" Grayson shrank back. "Sorry. I won't bring up the kiss again. Just please put your look away."

"Do not tell *anyone* about that kiss, Grayson North! I only did it to keep us safe."

"He already told me," Mason's voice echoed in their earpieces.

Lucy groaned. "You may have superpowers, a magic tower, and a genius brother who can read books for you. And you may be my only hope to save my father, Grayson North..."

"This is going to be quite a 'but.'" Grayson frosted away more hypno-fire.

"*But* I want to keep one thing straight..."

Suddenly, Grayson spotted a fiery streak swooping around the John Hancock Building.

"I am *not* interested in you that way. So just keep your icy hands to yours—"

Grayson iced up his protective armor, grabbed Lucy's arm, and twirled her in front of him.

"Ah! What did I just—"

A streak of fire cut across the concrete. Grayson rocketed them down the street on an ice slick and swerved to avoid the blast.

"I promise!" Grayson shouted over Lucy's screams. He steered with the beam of his Frost-Blade and used his other hand for propulsion, just like on the water. "I will *never* touch you, unless I have to save your life."

Lucy wrapped her arms around Grayson's torso. She peeked over his shoulder.

Grayson focused on the road ahead. "What do you see?"

"Three of them," she shouted into his ear. "The ones with the wings!"

"Mace!" Grayson shouted. "We've got three Sulfurian waifs in hot pursuit! What does the book say about these guys? Any special weaknesses?"

"Checking!" came Mason's voice. "Hang on!"

Twin streaks of fire carved an X across Grayson's path. He swerved onto the street. Lucy tightened her grip.

"Pardon me! Frost-Keeper, coming through!"

A taxi driver yelled out his window as Grayson cut him off.

"Sorry!" Grayson said. "Special emergency! Kinda in a rush!"

A snarling jack-o'-lantern face stretched alongside him. Hot air pulsed as the waif beat fiery wings.

Grayson veered over the median into the opposite lane, spraying frost at the Sulfurian, forcing them both into oncoming traffic. A double-decker bus honked; Grayson dodged it.

Before the Sulfurian could reorient, he collided with the grill of the bus and ricocheted into a mailbox. Grayson glanced back. Orange embers puffed into the air amid scores of burning letters. "Sorry, Post Office!"

Lucy shouted, "Grayson, look out!"

He glanced forward, swerved, and narrowly avoided an oncoming cab. Then he jetted to the right side of the road.

"Waifs prefer to attack from the sky," came Mason's voice.

"Obviously!" Lucy shouted.

Mason continued. "They fly using currents of hot air…"

Fireballs rained in front of them. Grayson veered between the blasts. *I'm lucky there aren't as many cars out as normal,* he thought. *Hard enough to keep us safe, and keep this ice-slick going, let alone try to counterattack.*

"Get to the river," Mason advised. "The journal says to attack from underneath. Get them close to water, then use ice geysers to take them by surprise."

"Ice geysers?" Lucy asked.

Fire exploded in their path. Grayson didn't have time to dodge the blast. Instead, he constructed an impromptu ice ramp. They slid and launched into the air over the wall of flames. For one horrifying moment, they somersaulted in freefall.

Instinct took over. Grayson spotted a fire hydrant at the curb. In a split second, he fired a blast of cold that expanded the hydrant and popped its valves.

White water sprayed into the street. Grayson reached for the gushing streams and summoned spirals of liquid towards them.

He and Lucy landed faceup as an ice slide froze beneath them. The chute extended over the sidewalk, toward the river. "Hang on!" Grayson shouted.

Lucy grabbed Grayson's torso. Blasts of fire cut through the sky. They slipped over the guard rail and plummeted toward the rippling blue-green surface of the Chicago River.

Grayson summoned coils of river water to connect with their frozen chute. They bulleted down the ramp. Before they reached the bottom, Grayson got to his feet, froze the surface of the river, and made a wide ice floe.

Lucy spun past him, but he caught her hand before she reached the edge of the floe. Grayson helped her stand up.

"How did you do all of that?"

Grayson shrugged. "Instinct. Like earlier today when I fought Scarlet Fury and saved Mason over the lake. I sort of let my inner Frost-Keeper guide me."

Lucy pointed at the silhouettes of three waifs soaring over the bridge.

"Hang tight," Grayson said.

Lucy locked her arms around Grayson as he ice-surfed them under the bridge. The Sulfurians' glowing reflections rippled. Bat-winged shadows swooped toward the water. Bright orange faces gleamed against the waves.

Grayson made a U-turn beneath the bridge. As he turned, he dropped twin blasts of icy energy on either side of him.

The Sulfurian waifs swooped down, breathed fire in an X pattern, and missed. Just as they flapped to change directions, Grayson's time-delayed cold bombs erupted into pillars of ice behind him.

Grayson swerved into the shade of the Michigan Avenue Bridge and watched as spires of ice swelled and entrapped the two waifs. Icy geysers stabbed their attackers. Icicles erupted from the waifs' bodies, like frozen sea urchins.

The waifs wailed, the fire in their mouths died away, and they splattered into glittering clouds of snow.

"Yes!" Grayson said. "Eat Frost-Keeper depth charges, freaks!"

"Grayson!" Lucy shoved him aside as the third Sulfurian's white hot breath scorched above. Grayson plummeted underwater. He kicked up and spotted Lucy swimming toward him.

The final Sulfurian swooped. Its jagged mouth blazed.

Grayson created an ice raft for Lucy with frozen handles. "Hang onto that!"

Lucy yelped as Grayson summoned arctic wind to push her toward an emergency ladder. The waif faltered and spiraled out of control.

Air currents, Grayson remembered. *They use heat for lift.* Grayson's arctic wind had been intended to guide Lucy to safety, but it also disrupted the waif's flight path.

The waif righted himself and spat a fireball. Grayson dunked underwater and covered himself in an icy shelter as fire burst above his head.

He launched himself toward the surface on an ice pillar and rocketed onto another ice slick. The waif snarled and chased. He spotted Lucy, swimming for the edge.

Good, he thought. *She's at a safe distance. I can cut*

loose!

Grayson harnessed another gust of cold. He turned and charged the waif. His opponent tumbled and faltered on frigid air. Grayson slid beneath him, summoned an icy pillar beneath his feet and shot upward. He thrust the Frost-Blade and impaled the waif, skewering him into the bottom of the Michigan Avenue Bridge.

The waif's white hot eyes went black. Smoke billowed from his mouth as he crystalized. Grayson slid down his pillar, like a fire pole, as the waif burst into snowflakes.

He made a new ice slick and checked for any more Sulfurians in the vicinity, then he glided back toward Lucy. Lucy struggled up a metal ladder.

"Need a hand?"

Lucy shivered. "I am freezing. And I am terrified. And I am worried sick that you are going to fall and break your neck every time you do something crazy!" She extended her hand. "And yes, of course I need a hand!"

"No problem. Sorry about all the cold." He helped Lucy up. "But, you know, you're welcome."

"*Merci beaucoup*," Lucy said softly. She looked over Grayson. "Are you okay?"

"Sure," he said. *Just having a hard time understanding if you're angry, or stressed, or grateful, or all of the above.*

Before he could ask, Lucy gripped his wrist. Sharp wing flaps echoed above the deserted streets: more waifs! Grayson's icy pillars rocked and slowly melted between the waves. Finally, one of them toppled and splashed.

"Down there!" came a scratchy yell.

"The river isn't safe, Mace," Grayson said. "We

need cover."

"Grayson, look!" Lucy pointed.

Grayson's jaw dropped as a coppery-silver keyhole formed, right in the brick of the Riverwalk. "Unbelievable."

"What is it?" Mason asked.

"A way out, let's hope!" Grayson retracted his Frost-Blade and raced toward the wall with his key. He turned the Frost-Key, and another opening appeared in the brick, just like the one at the Water Tower.

Inside, an icy blue cavern glowed. "Quick!" Grayson ushered Lucy in and followed. Grayson heard beating wings as the brick slid shut behind them.

Chapter 21

Lucy shivered as they hurried down the mysterious escape tunnel. "Why is it freezing in here?"

"Frost-Keeper, Frost-Key, Frost-Blade, ice powers. It's kind of a theme, if you haven't noticed." The Frost-Key transformed into a flashlight, and Grayson illuminated the steamy blue corridor.

"I'm going to catch pneumonia on the hottest day of July," Lucy complained.

"Better than being burned alive, princess," Grayson snapped. "Look, sorry my dead penguin lips are cold, and my lifesaving ice slides are cold, and that apparently my key unlocks convenient safety tunnels, but the catch is that, yes, *they're cold.*"

Lucy's teeth chattered. "I'm sorry, really! I *am* grateful. But I need a change of clothes."

"And a change of attitude, maybe," Grayson said. "Ever since you met me, you've been looking down on me, and I thought maybe, after saving your life ten times in a row, you'd respect me or something."

"I said, I'm sorry! Learn to accept an apology! You're so stubborn."

"I am not! You're stubborn!"

Lucy huffed. "Now you are being stubborn *about* being stubborn!"

"I..." Grayson groaned. "I don't know how to argue against that! But seriously, come on, a little more gratitude!"

"I will give you all the gratitude you want, once I am warm and my father is safe," Lucy said. "You can name your price."

Grayson's heart sank. "Name my price?"

"Yes. Whatever you want."

"I..." Grayson melted the ice from his face. He shook his head. "You think I want money? You think I'm helping you because you're rich?"

"I'm not stupid. And I do not care. My father will give anything if you can save him and his hotel."

"I'm not doing this for money, Lucy. I'm doing this because it's the right thing to do. And..."

"And?"

"And I like you."

Lucy's stern expression melted away.

"Hey, you guys," Mason's voice interrupted. "Where are you?"

"In some weird tunnel that opened along the river," Grayson answered. "It was like the Frost-Key generated an escape for us. You want to look into that, Mace? I'd appreciate it, because I'm a *grateful* person."

"Uh... no problem."

"See!" Grayson scowled at Lucy. "That's gratitude."

"You are so arrogant," Lucy seethed through chattering teeth. "If you were really so gracious, you would have thanked Mason for the lifesaving advice he fed you earlier. You would have thanked *me* for pushing you out of the way of that Sulfurian you completely missed on the river. Do not try to shame me, Grayson North!"

"Fine!" Grayson's voice echoed down the tunnel. "Thanks all around! Thank you, Lucy! Thank you, Mason! Thank you, dead Frost-Keeper who forced this terrifying burden on me!"

Lucy glared for a moment, then she twisted away, arms folded in anger.

Mason cut in again: "Everything okay, Gray?"

He took a deep breath. "Yeah, sorry... just a little stressed. What've you got for us?"

"The book shows a map of access tunnels that run along a 'trans-dimensional axis,'" Mason explained. "They're not exactly shortcuts, but they allow you to sneak through the city without being seen. Some of them connect back to the Water Tower. That's good, because sooner or later someone would notice you going in and out that back door."

"Check the tunnel that starts at the Michigan Avenue Bridge," Grayson said. "We need to know where it leads."

"One sec."

After a moment, Grayson added. "Thank you, Mason."

Lucy turned and sighed. Breath steamed into a frosty cloud that obscured her face. "Why do you like me?" she asked.

"Good question!" Grayson said. "I'm second guessing the whole thing."

"Because I'm pretty?"

"Not gonna lie, that got my attention. But I didn't really start liking you until we were talking by the Riverwalk. I could tell how much you missed your mom and your home and your friends. How hurt you were when your dad yelled at you. I know how that feels."

"You do?"

"Yes," Grayson said. "I got in a big fight with my older brother Jason today. Well, several fights. Okay, the whole summer has been like one long, never-ending fight with Jason."

"About your parents' divorce?"

"They're not getting divorced! It's a rocky patch," Grayson insisted. "But yeah. We fight about that. We fight about our dad. Jason's always riding me at work, even though I do a good job. He never listens to me. It's just…"

"It's just what?"

"Until this summer, Jason was my hero. I always wanted to be like him. Jason went to school, so I wanted to go to school. Jason rode a bike, so I wanted to. Jason got a car, and I was all into cars. Jason got a job, and I was so excited that I was going to have one too. This summer, in that one way, it was like I finally caught up with Jason, you know? I thought we'd be like equals. But he reminds me every day that we're not. That I'll never be as cool or attractive or popular or smart or any of the things that make Jason perfect."

"Nobody is perfect," Lucy said.

"Nice try. I saw you gushing over him when he spewed all that French."

Lucy paused. "Your brother is handsome, but he is also older. Some day you will, perhaps, be slightly less ugly than you are now." The white steam cleared, and Grayson saw the teasing smile on her face.

"Ha, ha. Only slightly, huh?"

"We will have to wait and see." She smiled through chattering teeth. "But if Jason was so perfect, then *he* would be the Frost-Keeper."

Grayson smiled.

"You guys are in luck," Mason said through the earpiece. "It's hard to say for sure where the tunnel led in Drake's time, but based on online maps, I think it's taking you to the Red Line tunnel by the Slynt. You should be able to get to the lobby without any more waifs spotting you."

"Awesome," Grayson said. "Now all we have to do is worry about the Sulfurians waiting at the hotel."

Chapter 22

Grayson and Lucy reached the end of the icy tunnel, and the wall split open. They emerged under the escalator in the commuter tunnel—close to where Grayson had received the Frost-Key that morning. The wall slid shut behind them.

Lucy shivered as they rode the escalator toward the hotel lobby. "I need a change of clothes," she said. "Meet me in the lobby in ten minutes."

"We shouldn't split up," Grayson said.

"You are *not* coming to my room while I change!"

"Not what I meant!" Grayson sighed. "Okay. Ten minutes. Be careful. If you run into trouble, tell me and Mason over the headset, cool?"

"Agreed."

Lucy hid her face as she passed the reception desk. Her shoes clanked over the metal Slynt emblem as she headed toward the elevators.

"I should check on Aunt Linda, Mace," Grayson whispered. "And Jason too, I guess. I still want to know why my powers weren't working around him."

"I'll look into it," Mason said. "Over and out!"

Grayson rounded the corner toward Linda Liu's Something Suite.

Someone grabbed his shoulder from behind. "Grayson."

Grayson spun and raised his flashlight.

"Whoa!" Officer Lucas held up his hands defensively. "Something wrong, Grayson?"

"Sorry!" Grayson exhaled relief. "I didn't know it was you."

"My shift ended, and I thought I'd stop by and, uh—" he smiled sheepishly and scratched the back of his neck— "maybe get your aunt's autograph? Is she around?"

"Sure! In fact, I was just heading over there. But, hey, can I ask you something first?"

"Anything."

"Has it seemed like kind of a weird day to you?" Grayson studied Officer Lucas's face.

"You know, it's odd that you say that, Grayson. Ever since this morning... and then the museum fire, and the harbor fire... well." He stared blankly. Then he glanced back at Grayson and smiled.

"Yeah?" Grayson asked. "You were saying? Something about odd fires?"

"I was saying something?" He shook his head. "Only that I'd love to have your Aunt Linda's autograph."

"Officer Lucas, did you look at one of those weird swirly fireballs outside? Did you see swirling flame on the news, or online, or at the police station?"

Recognition flickered in Officer Lucas's eyes.

"Don't you think it's weird that there are so few people out downtown on a Saturday?" Grayson asked.

The officer furrowed his brow. "Come to think of it..." He smiled blankly. "Not really."

"Okay then." Grayson sighed. "Aunt Linda's probably in the kitchen getting ready for Mr. Slynt's engagement banquet. Wait here a sec."

"Sure, Grayson." Officer Lucas smiled and checked his phone. Out of the corner of his eye, Grayson caught a bright, orange icon on the screen.

"Mason," Grayson whispered as he headed toward the kitchen. "I need you to research those fire mages. They are making people really stupid."

"Copy that," Mason said. "Figure out how to remove the germ from Slynt's brain, how to stop your powers from zonking out, how to cure the hypno-fire." He sighed. "Need anything else?"

"Yes," Grayson said. "Wish me luck." Grayson greeted the evening scoopers at the ice cream shop, slipped behind the counter of Something Suite, and pushed his way into the kitchen.

Utensils clinked, voices shouted, and pans clanked throughout the stainless-steel kitchen. Scents of fresh produce, simmering sauces, and browning meats blended as he passed counters and workstations. Chefs and kitchen workers called his name. Grayson smiled and waved politely. He scanned the room for Aunt Linda.

On the far side of the kitchen, Jason chopped vegetables. The scowl on his brother's face—directed right at him—made his skin creep. *What is your problem, Jason?* he wondered. *And more importantly, how come when the Sulfurians mind-wiped everyone else, Jason stayed mad?*

"Looking for your aunt?" one of the kitchen workers asked.

Grayson broke away from Jason's glare. "Yeah, Ramone. You seen her?"

"In the ballroom, talking to some higher-ups. How come you're not helping out tonight? Good tips at a fancy party like this!"

"I'm sort of already working overtime," Grayson explained. "Thanks!"

He headed past the steakhouse door, toward the ballroom. Aunt Linda was also approaching the ballroom doors, followed by Slynt's fiancée, Joanna Crisp. Two security guards with paper white hair and coal black shades flanked Joanna. Grayson moved closer to hear their conversation.

"Of course, it's your party, and... we'll do whatever we can," Aunt Linda stammered. "But Joanna, Something Suite is a staple of the hotel. I assumed an ice cream sundae would be a great nod to the brand, not to mention that we're in the middle of a heatwave."

Grayson froze. He squeezed his flashlight.

Joanna's cold, glazed eyes tilted at Grayson. "I hate to be a bother with last minute changes, Linda," she said. "I know what it's like to have a little pest come and start spoiling things. It's just that my friends and I absolutely *detest* cold desserts."

Her two guards smirked.

"Nobody is being a pest," Aunt Linda assured her. "We'll set aside some hot apple cobbler. Just give my head server a list based on the seating chart. We'll add the option; it's no problem."

"That's so generous, Linda," Joanna said. "A warm dessert for a warm occasion."

Grayson scowled at the Sulfurian woman. *This isn't about dessert,* he thought. *You're sending me a message. You've got my family right where you want them.*

Joanna smiled. *Very perceptive, Frost-Keeper.*

Grayson's heart skipped a beat. Joanna had spoken inside his head.

"Sorry to keep you, Linda. Goodness, I only have minutes to get ready and meet Alex for press time. I'm sure you have a thousand tasks to complete as well!" Joanna turned away and headed to the ballroom.

"Please, Joanna, if there's anything else we can do, don't hesitate," Aunt Linda said.

"You've done so much already." Joanna's attendants held the door for her. "The evening's going to be explosive! I just know it!" She gave one last wicked smile to Grayson and slipped into the ballroom.

"Witch," Grayson muttered.

Aunt Linda furrowed her brow and rushed past.

"Aunt Linda, hang on!" He hurried alongside her.

"Grayson, I'm so sorry, but Slynt's fiancée just threw a huge wrench into the whole evening! She wants hot cobbler for who even knows how many of her weird friends."

"How about a pointy popsicle through her heart?" Grayson snapped.

"Be nice, Gray. If tonight goes well, they'll ask me to cater the wedding, and it'll be the highest profile function of my career."

"Aunt Linda, can we talk? I need you to stay away from—"

"After midnight tonight, you can talk my ear off, Gray. Unless you know how to make cobbler?"

"I—"

"Of course you don't. Ramone! Take Jason and prep enough apple cobbler to feed—I don't know—fifty?"

"Aunt Linda—"

"Where's Mason?"

"Close by. But you know that cop I was telling you about? He wants to meet you. He's in the lobby."

"Ah! Grayson, this is the worst time! Give him a coupon to the steak house or something. Tell him to come back."

"But it's more than that, it's…"

Aunt Linda finally stopped and locked eyes with him. "Gray? Is everything all right?"

Grayson suddenly realized that Joanna's two shaded goons were still flanking the ballroom door. Jason was still glaring at him.

Joanna's voice suddenly echoed in his mind: *What could you possibly tell her, Frost-Keeper? Even if she believed you, my eyes are everywhere.*

The guards by the doorway held up their hands. Hypno-fire swirled over their palms, and Grayson averted his eyes.

I will rewrite their minds. Turn them all against you.

"Grayson?" Aunt Linda said. "What's wrong?"

"Nothing. Sorry I bothered you. I just… Officer Lucas is really nice."

"That's sweet. Tell him I'm sorry. Have him stop by again, on a weekday afternoon, when I'm not having a dessert apocalypse."

"I wish it was just a dessert apocalypse," Grayson muttered.

"Stick with Mason tonight," Aunt Linda said. "Don't leave the hotel." She tasted a huge pot of sauce with a wooden spoon. "More garlic!"

"Okay," Grayson said dejectedly. He shook his head at the two Sulfurians by the door.

Leave this hotel, Frost-Keeper, came Joanna's voice. *You don't want a fight here.*

No, you don't, Grayson thought. *Because it's more for you to cover it up with your mind voodoo. Do you think I care?*

You care about your loved ones. Joanna's smoky laughter scratched at the inside of Grayson's skull. *Leave us be. Or better yet, stay for the party.*

You want a temporary truce, fine, Grayson thought. *But first, tell your stupid goons to stay out of the kitchen. If I see any of your people near my family, I swear, I will stab them.*

Laughter crackled in Grayson's mind. *Very well, Frost-Keeper.*

The two Sulfurian guards tipped their shades to show Grayson their blazing yellow eyes. Then they slipped into the ballroom.

We have a gift for you, The Sulfurian echoed. *But as I said, there's still so much to do. Run along, boy.*

Grayson hurried back into the lobby. He almost collided with Officer Lucas after he rounded the counter. "Oh! Hey, I'm really sorry, but—"

"She's busy." Officer Lucas nodded. "No worries, Grayson. I get it."

"No, you should come back another time. It's just that there's this engagement party." *And these monsters, and maybe the second Great Chicago Fire...*

"Sure." Officer Lucas smiled and headed toward the exit.

"Hey, Officer Lucas!" Grayson hurried after him. "Quick question. Purely hypothetical."

He paused by the door. "Shoot."

"What if you know something really bad is going to happen, but there's no way to warn anyone?"

"Then you need proof."

"But what if something else is stopping them from understanding? Like you know, people who are suppressing evidence or silencing witnesses or whatever. How do cops handle problems like that?"

Officer Lucas rubbed his chin. "Wow, that's a very good question, Grayson. First, I would say you can't solve every problem all at once. Big problems don't work that way. Sometimes you have to prioritize and do the next best thing. Moment by moment."

"What if every 'next best thing' you try blows up in your face?"

"Keep doing the right thing. Sooner or later, at least *some* people will notice. The best thing anyone can be is an example."

Grayson nodded.

"If you have even one ally who *already* believes you, then open yourself up to that person's help. You can always talk to your brother, or your aunt, or your parents, a friend. Or a cop." Officer Lucas gave a thumbs up. "If something is going on, Grayson, you can trust me."

I do, Grayson thought. *I just need you to stop looking at that stupid hypno-fire.* "Thanks. Be careful out there."

"Always. See you later, Grayson."

As Officer Lucas headed out, Grayson processed his advice. *I do have two good allies, Mason and Lucy. So how can they help me best?*

He lowered his voice, "Mason, I think I might be pulling you in too many directions. For now, just focus on the fire mages. Once we counter their stupid hypno-fire, more people will believe us, and then we can focus on other goals, okay? One thing at a time."

"Roger that," Mason said. "Good point."

Suddenly, a loud crash sounded in Grayson's earpiece, followed by glass breaking. An angry man shouted in French, *"Tu es une fille très terrible!"*

Lucy shouted back in French. Grayson listened closely. There was a cold, calculating quality to the male voice.

"It's her dad," Grayson whispered. "Lucy's in trouble!"

Chapter 23

Grayson bolted through the lobby, past the front desk. His shoes clanked over the coppery Slynt emblem in front of the elevators.

"Hey!" Came a voice from the front desk. "Stop right there!"

Grayson hit the Up button on the elevator and waited.

"You're Linda Liu's nephew from Something Suite."

Grayson groaned and faced the angry manager, the same guy who had thrown a fit over the ice in the lobby.

"You can't be running around the hotel like a madman!"

"I do not have time for this," Grayson muttered. The elevator slid open behind him.

"Well, you better make time!"

"What floor is the Slynt Penthouse?" Grayson asked.

The manager seemed taken aback. "It's a private floor, and you don't have access. What business do you think you have with Mr. Slynt, exactly?"

Grayson took one step backward into the elevator. "I'm saving his daughter's life." He swirled a huge snowball on his hand behind his back and then whipped it at the manager's face.

The manager stumbled back in surprise. He spat snow and cleaned his glasses.

"Really sorry!" Grayson hit the Close button and pressed the highest available floor.

"I'm calling security!" The manager's voice muffled behind the doors as the elevator ascended.

"Mace, any idea what floor the Slynts would be on? I'm guessing the top, but..." Grayson glanced down at his Frost-Key. The tip had transformed into a flat metal rectangle. Grayson glanced over at a keycard slot labeled *Penthouse Level.*

"Never mind," Grayson slipped his key into the electronic slot, pulled it out, and hit the penthouse button.

"I've got intel, Gray," Mason said. "The Sulfurians have a hive culture, like bees or ants, where the different castes perform different jobs. The Grand Sulfurian is the big boss, but there's also a commander in charge of each class."

"Makes sense," Grayson said. "Scarlett Fury is in charge of the warriors and drones. Blood-Wing is the head waif."

"And Joanna is the head fire mage," Mason said. "She's in charge of manipulating the media, the authorities, and civilians, to keep humans from noticing what the Sulfurians are doing. In Victor Drake's time, the head mage worked for the newspaper."

"Let's not forget, Joanna's also in charge of making me look crazy," Grayson said. "Gotta love that."

"Here's the good news," Mason continued. "The mages are all connected. They're like the frontal lobe of the hive mind."

"What does that mean?"

"It means Joanna channels her powers *into* her minions. Every fireball or image of a fireball that carries their subliminal control depends on Joanna's focus and willpower."

"So you're saying once you take out the head mage, it'll break the spell citywide. That *is* good news. But they have every human in this hotel hostage. How do I get close enough to take her out?"

"Find a way," Mason said. "If you stop Joanna, we'll expose the Sulfurians to the whole city."

The elevator neared the penthouse, Floor 88. "I lost audio on Lucy," Grayson whispered. "Did you hear anything since they started yelling in French?"

"Nothing," Mason said. "Be careful."

Gilded doors slid open, revealing a marble hall with white pillars. Brass planters burst with exotic plants and flowers, like a Roman garden. A sculpted fountain with angels spewed water into a reflecting pool in front of a gigantic mirror.

Grayson inched down the penthouse hallway and peeked around a corner. Two security guards in shades flanked double-glass doors into an expansive living area with posh furniture.

These guards must be Sulfurian, Grayson thought. *But how can I be sure?*

In response to his thoughts, his vision blurred into a colorful spectrum. The marble floor and walls glowed a cool blue color. The air conditioning ducts were icy black.

Nice! he thought. *Thermal vision!*

The guards' bodies glowed orange and red in the

legs and arms, but in their cores, by the heart and brain, they were blazing with unnaturally white-hot energy.

Definitely Sulfurian, Grayson thought. *So, what's the best plan of attack here? Rush in, sword swinging? Every time I use my powers it just attracts more Sulfurians.*

Grayson extended his Frost-Blade. He tapped it on the ground until the thermal outlines of the Sulfurians exchanged glances. One nodded at the other and headed down the hall to investigate.

Grayson ducked behind an antique planter and a leafy green fern. The Sulfurian scanned the foyer, then headed toward the elevator. Grayson's thermal vision faded. Through the leafy brush, he made out the faint glow under the Sulfurian's shades.

As soon as his enemy stepped into range, Grayson jabbed his sword up, through the guard's heart. The Sulfurian gave a stifled cry, frosted over, and burst into powdery snow.

The second Sulfurian hurried down the hall. He rounded the corner and reached for his radio. Fire sputtered beneath his shades, and he started to yell. Grayson swiped his Frost-Blade and coated the marble floor in a slick patch of ice. The Sulfurian yelped as he slipped onto his back, dropping the radio.

Grayson blasted at the floor, and a thick ice spike stabbed upward, impaling the Sulfurian. Frost spread from his chest, and he splattered into a carpet of snow.

Grayson examined the frosty remains on the marble floor. *I don't want to leave a mess like last time.*

Grayson concentrated. The ice and snow swirled

into a sub-zero cyclone of arctic wind. He directed the swirling cold down the hall and deposited the frozen remains into the fountain water.

"Two Sulfurians down, Mace. Heading into the penthouse."

Grayson crept toward the double doors, cautiously opened one side, and slipped in. Classical piano music wafted from speakers in the ceiling. Another marble fountain trickled by an ornate bathroom entranceway. Grayson glanced right into a white marble kitchen with cherry wood cabinets. To the left, an oak dining room table sprawled beneath a crystal chandelier. Enormous windows overlooked the river and the skyline.

Grayson slipped through the dining room. A spiral staircase curled up to a second landing. Oil paintings of European countrysides covered one wall.

Grayson nearly jumped when he noticed a man with white streaked hair, standing perfectly still. He was resting his knuckles on a console table lined with liquor bottles. His eyes were closed. It was Alexander Slynt.

Slynt's face was weary. He slowly raised his hands and massaged his temples.

Where's Lucy? Grayson wondered. An unpleasant shiver prickled his spine. *How far gone is her dad? What could Joanna or the germ in his head drive him to do to his own daughter?*

Grayson inched closer. He held his key ready. *I still don't know how I'm supposed to handle this.* His heart thundered. *What do I do to cure him? Should I try to restrain him until we figure this out?*

Grayson neared Slynt. Suddenly, strong arms grabbed and spun him around. Grayson shouted. A massive fist squeezed his wrist.

Grayson cried out and dropped his metal ice cream scooper.

"You!" The hulking Mr. Cortez loomed over him.

Grayson struggled and shouted. He reached for his scooper, but Cortez grabbed his other arm and held him still. "Linda Liu's nephew! What are you doing up here?"

"Let go of me you hypno-monster-psycho!" Grayson yelled. "Leave Mr. Slynt alone!"

"*Me* leave him alone?" Cortez growled. He held Grayson's wrist tight with one hand. Then he reached up and lifted his shades with the other, revealing incredibly angry, but completely normal human eyes. "You have a serious misunderstanding about who is the intruder here, young man!"

"I agree!" Slynt shouted. "I would absolutely love to know what is going on here!"

Cortez spun Grayson around so that he was facing the cold, calculating eyes of Lucy's father.

"How did this boy get past security?" Slynt asked.

"I didn't see any guards," Grayson lied. "They must be slacking off."

Cortez spun Grayson around again and yelled in his face. "You are facing serious trespassing charges, kid!"

Grayson carefully studied Cortez's eyes a second time. They were huge, white and angry, with eyebrows scrunched with rage, but there wasn't even a flicker of fire behind them. "Cortez is human," Grayson said, for his brother's sake. "I would have bet money he wasn't."

"Of course, he's human!" Slynt snapped. "What are you implying, young man?"

"He is implying that Mr. Cortez is behaving like a rabid beast," came Lucy from the top of the stairs.

"Unhand my friend. Now."

Lucy's hair had been blown dry, freshly styled, and intricately arranged over her shoulders like a blond waterfall. She was decked out in an ice-blue sleeveless dress, with a diamond studded purse over her shoulder and matching blue high heels.

"This boy is trespassing," Cortez growled.

"Nonsense. I invited him," Lucy insisted. "As my plus one."

"Really?" Grayson said. "I mean, yeah, definitely. I'm Lucy's date."

Lucy glared. "My *platonic* plus one." Lucy gracefully descended the spiral steps. "Did you not hear me the first time, Cortez? Unhand him."

Cortez scowled and released Grayson. He rubbed his wrist and snatched the metal scooper off the ground.

"I refuse to attend your engagement party unless Grayson North has a seat at our table," Lucy said. "That is all that I ask."

Slynt frowned. "What is this about, Lucienne? Are you so insistent upon being disagreeable that you would make me invite this hoodlum to the most high-profile event of the year?"

"I'm not a hoodlum," Grayson snapped.

Slynt stepped up to Grayson and sized him up. He sniffed and made a disgusted face. "He smells like the river!" He glared.

Grayson studied Slynt's eyes for any signs of a fiery glow, but he too looked completely normal. Thermal vision filtered over Grayson's vision, and he confirmed that both men were entirely human. *Would the germ be hot?* he wondered. *Or is it inactive?*

"Did you take my daughter swimming in the

Chicago River?" Slynt's voice was icier than the Frost-Blade.

"Um... in fairness, she pushed me in first," Grayson said.

"He's a punk!" Slynt snapped. "I won't allow it."

Lucy shrugged. "Then I will not attend."

"How does that make me look if my own daughter, who flew in from Paris, refuses to attend our engagement dinner? If none of my children are present to celebrate?"

Lucy shrugged. "Tell them I'm ill."

"I'm sorry if you want to go trouncing around with this river-rat, Lucy. But we have obligations."

She folded her arms and unleashed *the look* on her father. The same look she gave Grayson when she insisted on staying with him.

"I have asked so little of you since you arrived. It's just *one* dinner." Slynt's voice bubbled with suppressed rage. His eyes narrowed like daggers, and Grayson suddenly realized where his daughter had learned *the look*.

"All I ask is *one* guest," Lucy said. "At your *one* dinner."

Slynt's blond assistant Wesley marched into the room, sporting a sleek blue blazer, checking off items on his tablet. "Mr. Slynt, we have a photo op with Joanna and the hotel board in—"

"Tell them to wait, Wesley! Lucy, I won't have this smelly, rabble-rousing kid at my party."

"Grayson is Linda Liu's nephew," Lucy said. "His aunt is good enough for your hotel. He should be good enough to spend an evening with your daughter."

Wesley made a pleased sound. "You know, that would make a good fluff piece: Alexander Slynt's daughter dates Cuisine Channel star's nephew.

Hashtag Grucy. Or maybe Luson? This is a fabulous idea, boss!"

Lucy smiled.

Slynt glared at Wesley. "Fine. Then *you* are in charge of cleaning this boy up and getting him appropriate dinner attire in the next thirty minutes, Wesley."

"I—what?" Wesley's eyes widened like a deer in headlights.

Slynt snatched Grayson by the collar. "And if you make even *one* faux pas at my engagement party, I will have your aunt out on the street. Do you understand?"

"Um..." Grayson gulped. "Actually, I do not know what 'faux pas' means."

"Explain it to him." Slynt shoved Grayson toward his assistant and stormed toward the exit. Cortez secured his shades over his eyes and followed.

Wesley sighed. "A faux pas is anything rude or inappropriate. In other words, keep your mouth shut, smile, behave, and listen to Uncle Wesley." He whipped out his smartphone. "What size tux are you, kid?"

"Dude! How would I know?"

"I'll find a tape measure." Wesley hurried into the other room.

Grayson smiled at Lucy. "Hey, dinner date! Quick thinking there."

"Do not get any ideas, Grayson North. I want you with me for protection, and so we can keep a close eye on Joanna and my father."

"Yeah, yeah, I'm with you. Totally a professional Frost-Keeper-focused job here." Grayson mused, "But what do you think of 'Gracy?' That's got a good ring to it."

Lucy shuddered. "If a tabloid merges our names as a result of this evening, I will never speak to you again!"

"Lucy, Grayson," Mason's voice cut into their earpieces. "If I heard all that right, you could be in serious trouble. Joanna and her Sulfurians are controlling this whole event. They'll have all the humans in that ballroom hostage, including Aunt Linda and Jason and the whole kitchen staff."

"That's why we have to stay close to the situation," Grayson said. "I'm the only person who has a shot at stopping these guys. Creepy old Joanna was taunting me earlier. Speaking right inside my head. She can't expect to threaten my family and just get away with it. Once we stop her, everyone will know what the Sulfurians are up to."

"But they know you're after her. That's why she's proceeding with this whole stupid dinner," Mason explained. "Gray, this is a trap."

Chapter 24

Grayson showered and refreshed himself in one of the penthouse's guest bedrooms. The adjoining bathroom was like a private luxury spa, with black tile, a Jacuzzi, and a huge shower with seven high-pressure jets. Grayson scrubbed away the stench of river water with fancy body wash that smelled like Jason's aftershave.

The Frost-Key shapeshifted into a metal comb that he used to brush his hair. A black tuxedo, white shirt, and polished piano-black shoes had been laid out on the bed.

Grayson dressed as far as he could, but by the time he had his shirt, pants, and jacket on, he realized there were several extra pieces and shiny buttons he couldn't quite figure out. He slipped his metal comb inside his interior coat pocket and opened the door to find Wesley texting up a storm.

"Hey, Wesley! I think I'm ready, but what are these extra thing-a-doobers?"

Wesley's look of abject horror made Grayson fear a Sulfurian was creeping behind him.

"What?" He glanced back. "What is it? How do I

look?"

Wesley sighed. "You look about six years early for junior prom. Come here." Wesley tucked his phone away and took the extra buttons from Grayson. He started to push them through the buttonholes of Grayson's shirt. "These are studs. Those are cuff links. I take it you have never tied a bowtie?"

"I've never tied *any* tie," Grayson boasted.

Wesley undid and redid Grayson's bowtie. "From food service to rubbing elbows with the rich and famous. You're the embodiment of the American Dream, kid. Speaking of which, where is that ice cream scooper you carry around like a security blanket?"

The Frost-Comb chilled against Grayson's heart. "I uh, put it away."

"Good. I don't want to see it at Mr. Slynt's party. You're going to be a perfect gentleman, tonight." Wesley straightened the bowtie. "What is it with you and that thing, anyway?"

"Family heirloom. I come from a long, proud line of dessert people."

"You culinary types. Be charming tonight, not weird, okay?" Wesley spun Grayson toward the full length mirror. "There!"

Grayson smiled at his reflection. He looked like a movie star or secret agent.

"Hm." Wesley crossed the room and snatched a tube of hair gel from the bathroom. He squirted some in his palm. Then he mussed up Grayson's hair and swept it into strategically placed spikes. "Perfect!"

Wesley gathered his tablet and briefcase and ushered Grayson down the spiral steps. Lucy paced the living room. Grayson cleared his throat, and she glanced up.

For one moment, her eyes widened, and the corners of her pink lips started to point into a smile, but then she cleared her throat, looked away and regained her cool composure. "You look acceptable."

"Acceptable? Please!" Wesley pushed Grayson closer to Lucy. "He's *Teen Beat* material. Not bad for a twenty-minute transformation. Thank you, Wesley. Oh, no problem, kids, that's what I'm here for—to give makeovers to ice cream boys. Hold still!"

Wesley spun Grayson around one last time and pinned a pale blue rose to his lapel. The flower matched the blue of Lucy's dress. "See, fairytales do come true." Wesley clapped his hands and ushered them toward the door. "Now let's go; we're late!"

Wesley answered his phone as the gold elevator doors slid shut. "Lucy and her date will be down in seventy-two seconds. Send press to the elevator. The kitchen needs to start hor d'oeuvres in four and a half minutes. Tell that hound from the Tribune he has thirty seconds in exactly five minutes with Marcy, but don't tell him I *said* he was a hound... that's not what happened last time, Steven!"

"Hey," Grayson whispered. "I know I'm only here to protect you, but... you look nice."

Lucy looked away. She whispered, "I am terrified. How are you so calm?"

He shrugged. "It's the Frost-Keeper's job to stay cool."

The elevator opened to the lobby. "Smile, kids!" Wesley guided them out onto the metal Slynt crest.

Lucy grabbed Grayson's arm and put on a perfect, winning smile. Grayson forced a wide grin. Bright camera flashes spotted his vision. Paparazzi shouted for Lucy's attention. And then suddenly, amid all of it, Grayson heard a horrible *prick-prock* that he could somehow pick out among all the high-heeled shoes in the lobby.

Scarlett Fury strutted up behind the paparazzi. Her ruby lips stretched into a sinister smirk. Bright fiery curls swirled over her shoulders. "What a hot couple!" she shouted.

Lucy squeezed Grayson's shoulder. Grayson reached into his jacket, felt the chill of the metal comb over his fingertips.

Scarlett Fury pushed her way to the front of the crowd.

"Back off," Grayson said, under his breath. "I'll skewer you."

Flashbulbs went off all around them. Reporters called for Lucy's attention.

Scarlett laughed. "Ooh! I'm shaking! You must think you're pretty fast, Frost-Keeper. By the time you get that little icepick of yours out, I'll have charred the flesh off all these reporters' bones."

Grayson's heart hammered. He wrapped his hand around the handle of the comb. Cold air steamed through his lips.

Scarlett Fury smiled, adjusted her shades, and started backing away into the crowd of reporters. "You'll be melting young hearts with these headlines, Frost-Keeper." Orange light flickered under her sunglasses. "Or maybe you'll just be melting. I guess we'll know by the end of the night."

She tossed her red locks and stalked back across the lobby. Between camera strobes, Grayson lost her in the crowd of partygoers.

"She didn't attack," Lucy whispered. "Why not?"

"Too many witnesses," Grayson guessed. "Especially with all those cameras going off. Sulfurians hate leaving evidence."

The photographers snapped their fingers and shouted Lucy's name. Grayson smiled and held Lucy's hands as she answered questions and posed with him.

Deep down, he couldn't shake Mason's warning that the evening was a trap. *She didn't attack because she's not afraid of me,* he realized. *Maybe whatever they have planned can't be stopped.*

Chapter 25

After their photo op, Grayson and Lucy explored the lobby, but found no sign of Scarlett or any other Sulfurians.

Mason cut in over their earpieces. "Drake's journal lists two key factors to hatching the germ. First, they need the negative emotions of a human host to incubate the germ. They also need to bathe that host in special radiation from their home dimension. The catch is, a human can't survive in their dimension, so the host has to remain here. It's why the Sulfurians work so hard to cover their tracks every century."

"They don't want humans to remember them and be prepared for next time," Grayson said. "So, they make the hatching germ look like a natural disaster, like a Great Fire."

Grayson flashed back to the fiery portal Scarlett Fury had opened that morning, and the blazing bearded face on the other side. "They're opening a portal," he said. "A big one! The adaptanium in the Slynt Tower must be designed to channel elemental energy from their dimension into ours."

"The same way your Frost-Key channels ice and

cold," Mason said.

"I don't think they'll hatch the germ here at the party," Grayson said. "Too many smartphones and reporters uploading live feed."

"Then we have to get to Joanna," Lucy said, "so you can break her spell over everyone."

"Careful," Mason warned. "If we do this wrong, all anyone will see is Grayson stabbing Mr. Slynt's fiancée. We have to get the Sulfurians to expose themselves first, then Grayson can stop Joanna. Either that, or you'll have to wait until you're alone with her."

Grayson sighed. "It couldn't just be easy."

They made their way past more reporters and guests through the grand archway to the ballroom.

Royal blue tablecloths were set with fine china, silver, and crystal glassware. Chandeliers shimmered in low lighting. A string quartet played romantic music while servers gracefully wove between guests balancing trays of appetizers and long-stemmed glassware.

"Wow!" Grayson marveled. "This is the swankiest thing I have ever done or probably ever will do."

"This is nothing," Lucy said. "You should have seen his eighth wedding in Peru."

"Invite me to his ninth if we survive," Grayson said. "Hopefully, it won't be Joanna."

"Lucienne! Oh, *bonjour!*" An older couple glided toward them. The man wore a black tux, and the woman was decked out in rubies that Grayson guessed could pay for his college education.

The woman kissed Lucy on both cheeks. "I don't know if you remember us, but I'm Mrs. Astor; my husband Vincent is an executive vice president. What a pleasure to have you in the States, dear!"

"*Oui*, madam." Lucy graciously shook both of their hands. "A pleasure to see you."

"And who is this charming gentleman?"

"He is—"

"Her date!" Grayson shook the woman's hand. "A superb pleasure to be here rubbing elbows." He hesitated. "We're not supposed to literally rub elbows, right?"

The woman laughed heartily. "How droll! You will have to tell me all about your schooling in Paris before the evening is through!"

Lucy excused them, and then shot Grayson her dagger eyes. "Next time, just let me speak."

"Good enough to stab your dad's fiancée, but not good enough to make small talk." Grayson rolled his eyes. "Got it."

Lucy opened her mouth to retort, but another couple approached and started to ask questions about her mother and Paris.

Grayson scanned the party for Sulfurians. He grinned when he spotted someone else. "Pardon me a moment, Ms. Slynt. I have to say hi to an old acquaintance."

Grayson approached a tall, dark-haired server carrying a shrimp cocktail platter. "Oh, *garçon!*" Grayson announced. "Kindly fetch me a Rob Roy, extra cherry juice, plenty of ice." He clapped his hands. "Make it snappy."

Jason turned and glared. He clenched his jaw and growled under his breath, "*What* are you *doing* in here?" His eyes widened. "Where did you get a tux?"

"I am Ms. Lucy Slynt's date," Grayson explained. "And that makes me a guest of this party, and it makes it *your* job to treat me well."

"You little liar," Jason snapped. "You're supposed

to be with Mason!"

"He's not a baby. He's perfectly safe. Safer than the rest of us, actually."

"Leave this party, right now," Jason said. "Get in the kitchen, before I lose my—"

Lucy took Grayson by the arm. "Grayson, may I speak with you, please?"

Jason's jaw dropped. His face flushed red.

"Oh, sure, Lucy. I'm sorry, this server was just giving me a hard time. He assumed I didn't belong at the party."

Lucy rolled her eyes. "I can't imagine why. Hello, Jason, good to see you." Then she said more urgently to Grayson, "Come with me *now*."

Grayson shouted over his shoulder as Lucy dragged him away. "I seriously want that Rob Roy!"

Jason shook his head and continued his rounds.

"What is it?" Grayson asked.

"The seating arrangement," she said. "Joanna rearranged it so that you'll be right next to her all through dinner."

Suddenly, the crowd broke into applause. Cameras strobed near the archway as Alexander Slynt and Joanna Crisp made an entrance. Once again, Joanna's vacant eyes turned and focused right on Grayson.

Welcome to my party, Frost-Keeper, her voice echoed in his mind. *If only these pathetic humans realized that you are the true guest of honor.*

Chapter 26

After cocktail hour, Grayson and Lucy took their seats at the head table. Mr. Slynt guided Joanna and sat her right next to Grayson. Slynt accepted a microphone and started to make a toast.

"You know there are so many ways to define progress." Slynt beamed at Joanna. "And when this wonderful woman walked into my office seven years ago with an incredible plan to build the world's most energy efficient skyscraper, right here in the heart of Chicago, I knew right away what an amazing business decision it would be to accept her proposal." He sighed. "But I had no idea how personally fulfilling it would be when she accepted mine."

The crowd gushed. Joanna held her hands over her heart and gave a warm smile.

Grayson directed his thoughts at the Sulfurian: *Is your plan to make me so disgusted that I puke at my first formal dinner party?* Grayson asked. *Because you're off to a good start.*

Slynt went on about how Joanna's vision had transformed his business, but his words were swallowed up by a strange crackling, like fire logs sputtering. Joanna's voice crept into his mind, smoky and dark. *Everything Alexander is saying is sincere, Frost-Keeper. He truly loves me.*

Your molten mumbo-jumbo is cooking his brains, and you know it! Grayson slipped his hand inside his jacket pocket. *Nobody could really love a poor man's stage hypnotist like you.*

You know so little, Frost-Keeper. A ruse so complex cannot be trusted to a mage's spell.

It's my first day. The metal comb chilled his fingers. *I'm learning as I go.*

Spells are good for short term diversion to cover up our Grand Leader's respawning. Your twenty-first century technology made that easier than ever.

Social media is a double-edged sword sometimes, Grayson thought.

Like the blade you plan to thrust through my burning heart? Mental laughter sizzled.

Grayson studied Joanna's milky-white eyes. "You're not really blind," he whispered aloud.

Joanna smiled sweetly. "I am sweetheart. Now please. My fiancé is giving a speech." She continued to cackle in his mind. *Do you not understand yet? I gave up my sight so that I could blend into this company for years, build this tower, and prepare everything for tonight. But when I sacrificed the fires of my true Sulfurian eyes, my second sight became more powerful than ever.*

The crowd burst into applause. Slynt had finished his speech. He joined Joanna on the other side of the table and kissed her. Joanna took the microphone from him. "May I say a few words?"

"Of course."

Joanna clasped her hands over her heart graciously and pretended to collect herself. "Firstly, thank you to all of our wonderful friends, family, and colleagues here with us today—" *It's the end of an era, Frost-Keeper.*

Chills ran down Grayson's spine as Joanna's speech blurred with her monstrous telepathic voice.

We are stronger and better equipped than ever to expand the Great Sulfurian Empire!

Lucy took Grayson by the arm and whispered. "Grayson, is everything okay?"

I see you shaking, sweating. Your hand trembling around that pathetic weapon in your coat pocket.

"Something's wrong," Grayson whispered to Lucy.

Skewer me on your Frost-Blade, Grayson North. Who among this crowd will believe a hyperactive, unruly child like yourself was doing anything but assaulting the fiancée of the world's most "—wonderful man!" Joanna gushed aloud. "And I am so blessed—" *with the honor of ending your pitiful lineage once and for all!*

"I'm not pitiful," Grayson growled under his breath.

You are an ignorant novice. The real-life Joanna smiled and applauded along with the crowd. The voice in Grayson's head grew louder, nastier. *You seek to suppress an inferno with a bucket of water. Pathetic.*

"You're the one who's pathetic," Grayson said. "I have you right where I want you!"

Lucy hushed Grayson as her father glared in their direction.

"Gray," Mason's voice sounded in his ear. "Who are you talking to?"

Check the exits, Frost-Keeper.

Grayson glanced behind him. Men and women wearing shades lurked at the edges of the ballroom.

A server in sunglasses hovered near the kitchen exit.

My true eyes are everywhere. She laughed. *Are you going to fight all of us? Here? How would that look if you made the first move? How many innocent people would burn due to your carelessness?*

"She's in my head," Grayson said. "Don't look, Lucy, but we're surrounded. Act normal."

Lucy furtively eyed the exits. She took a deep, nervous breath.

The end draws near, Frost-Keeper. I look forward to— "years of euphoria, with the man of my dreams." The crowd cheered. Slynt kissed his fiancée, to thunderous applause, and the band started to play dinner music.

Grayson whispered to Joanna as she sat. "Truce! Okay? Look." He removed his hand from his coat. "Not touching the Frost-Key. I won't attack if you won't attack. Okay?"

Joanna smiled sweetly and whispered. "You're a moth. Pathetic. Easily lured into my flame."

Grayson glanced back at the nearest exit. A Sulfurian drone in formalwear spread his palm open. Fire licked up and down his fingers.

"They're going to attack," Grayson whispered to Lucy.

A waiter served two covered platters in front of Grayson and Lucy. "Soup du jour?" The server wore black shades.

Before Grayson could react, the waiter lifted the metal coverings. Steam swirled from two piping hot bowls of soup and congealed in a glowing, fiery pattern underneath the covers.

"Don't look!" Lucy warned.

But ribbons of twisting molten light already held Grayson's gaze. He suddenly felt like he was floating in the center of the sun.

There we are, Frost-Keeper, Joanna's voice swallowed him like an ocean of lava. *Now you're deep, deep in my sway. You can't move. Can't even think unless I tell you to.*

Grayson's brain felt like a hunk of burning coal. Part of him knew he needed to touch the Frost-Key, feel the cold metal in his pocket and break the spell. But he had no sensation of even being in the ballroom anymore. He couldn't feel his jacket or the chair underneath him. Couldn't sense his arms or hands.

Surrender, Joanna commanded. *When I say the word, your eyes will be yours again, but your body will be mine. Do you understand?*

The furnace of Joanna's words overwhelmed him.

There is only one answer. Neon orange swirled around him. *And that answer is yes. When I say the word, your eyes will be yours again, but your body will be mine. Do you understand? Yes.*

Grayson struggled to think the word *No,* but it wouldn't come.

You will follow my Sulfurian attendants into the lobby, down, down into darkness, and wait for me at the bottom of this hotel. Do you understand?

"No!" Lucy's voice rattled Grayson's ears, jerked him awake. She was shaking him by the collar of his jacket. "Shut her out!" she shouted. "Grayson! Please!"

"Lucy!" Mr. Slynt shouted. He lowered his voice and growled in Grayson's ear. "What are you doing to my daughter, you hooligan?"

"I..." Grayson shook his head. The Sulfurian waiter grinned in front of him. A fireball reappeared on his hand. The skin under his shades glowed.

"Children!" Wesley appeared behind them.

"Behave."

"It's her!" Lucy pointed at Joanna. "Leave Grayson alone! Leave my father alone!"

The girl resisted again, Joanna's snide voice echoed in Grayson's mind. *She's stronger than you, Frost-Keeper. I should set her pretty hair on fire and end her.*

The fireball on the Sulfurian's palm swelled. He aimed at Lucy. Grayson spotted a bright red rectangle on the wall behind the head table.

The Sulfurian waiter jerked his fiery hand forward. Grayson pushed Lucy out of harm's way as a yellow streak flashed past his shoulder. Wesley shouted in surprise. Grayson darted toward the red fire alarm and slammed the handle.

Alarms blared.

Intense heat blazed on Grayson's shoulder. He blocked out the pain and yanked his flaming jacket off. He threw it on the table as it burned. A tuft of black smoke billowed toward the ceiling.

The sprinkler system activated.

Socialites, executives, and other partygoers leapt from their chairs. Jets of water sprayed down as panicked guests crowded toward the exits.

"What is happening? Oh, my goodness!" came Joanna's disoriented-sounding voice. Slynt and a few of their security guards rushed to her side and helped her away.

"You fire-flinging phony!" Grayson shouted.

Lucy poked her head out from under the table. "Are you okay?"

"I'm fine, just a mild shoulder char. Thanks for snapping me out of that." Grayson snatched his soaking wet, semi-burned coat off the sopping wet table. He fumbled through the pockets. "Come on, come on."

His heart sank, every pocket came up empty. "The Frost-Key!" He scoured the water-soaked ballroom. "We have to find it!"

The high pressure sprinkler system had drenched everyone, destroyed table settings, and ruined the food. Water pooled on the dance floor and sprayed the sound equipment.

"Lucy, you have to help me find my—"

Someone grabbed Grayson and hoisted him effortlessly into the air. Grayson shouted, certain it had to be a Sulfurian. But when he glanced downward, he found the furious, human eyes of Slynt's security guard, Mr. Cortez, poking over his shades. "You are coming with me. Now!"

Chapter 27

Cortez's iron grip dragged Grayson through puddles across the dance floor, toward the kitchen.

He shouted to Lucy. "Find the key, comb, whatever it is at the moment! Get to safety." He scanned the room for remaining Sulfurians but found none.

Cortez punched the kitchen doors open and dragged Grayson past the horrified staff.

"Mr. Cortez, listen!" Grayson said. "Didn't you notice that waiter with the sunglasses? He set my jacket on fire. I thought he was going to burn the whole place down. I was protecting people!"

Cortez shoved Grayson into Aunt Linda's office. "You are quite the storyteller. But as a matter of fact, *everyone* saw *exactly* what happened in there. You set your jacket on fire *after* you pulled the alarm!"

"They set me up! They wanted me to look stupid and make a scene. I did the only thing I could to clear the room. Ask Lucy!"

"Lucy is in trouble, too—with my boss. I could go on about what a serious offense this is..." Cortez leaned in and sneered. "But I'm not *your* boss, am I?" He nodded to the doorway.

Aunt Linda stood with her chef's hat clenched in her fist. Jason's shadowy figure loomed behind her.

"He's all yours." Cortez stormed past them.

Jason and Aunt Linda entered the office and shut the door. Jason crossed his arms and blocked the only exit.

"Please," Grayson took a deep breath. "Listen—"

"Grayson North," Aunt Linda's voice shook. "You have jeopardized my entire career. What possessed you to pull that alarm?"

Grayson stifled tears. "Aunt Linda, please, please believe me. What I'm about to say is weird, but—"

"No!" Jason shouted. "We are done listening to your insane explanations, Grayson. You have shamed our whole family."

"No, I haven't, Jace. Really." Tears finally broke free and streamed down his cheeks. He could deal with becoming a superhero overnight. He could deal with deadly fire monsters and wealthy executives in peril. What suddenly made him angrier than he had ever been was that the Sulfurians had turned his own family against him.

"How?" Jason shouted. "How can you defend this? Who put you up to it? Was it Lucy? Are you so dumb, so desperate to impress a pretty girl that you helped her wreck her dad's engagement party?"

"What?" Grayson shook his head. "Lucy didn't do anything wrong. Neither of us did! What's your problem, Jason?"

"*You* are the problem, Gray! We trusted you with the tiniest ounce of responsibility this summer, and you screwed up enough for a lifetime."

"All right!" Aunt Linda motioned for Jason to stop. "Jason, why don't you let me handle this."

"I'm sorry, but he needs to hear this," Jason's voice

came out stone cold. "Grayson, you always want to help out, but you never want to own up to anything. You can't even admit when you've done something wrong. You're like a... a parasite that pretends it's helping."

Grayson stood. "I *didn't* do anything wrong! And if you would listen instead of—"

"You know something?" Jason's face burned crimson. "You are *just* like Dad."

"Jason—" Aunt Linda started.

"Maybe that's not such a bad thing," Grayson yelled. "Maybe if you were more like Dad, you wouldn't have such a huge stick up your butt all the time. Dad's not a bully like you. He doesn't always assume the worst about me."

"You're always giving me your worst," Jason spat.

"Sure." Grayson sniffled. "I *always* screw up. Right?"

"Lately."

"Time out," Aunt Linda attempted to get between them.

Grayson shouted around her. "You're my older brother, Jason. You'd think you would look out for me, and pay attention, and have my back, on the one day I need it most! But why should I expect anything different. I've *always* had to figure everything out for myself. You've never really cared about—"

"Grayson, stop!" Aunt Linda placed her hands on his shoulders.

"You selfish little brat," Jason snapped. "Trying to tell me that I need to be a 'hero' like Dad? You want to know what a hero Dad is? What a great role model he is?"

Aunt Linda spun around. "Jason, settle down."

"Dad cheated on Mom. He's done it three times.

And thank God, this will be the *last* time, because once Dad is out of Mom's life, I hope he's out of *all* our lives. Forever."

Grayson's heart sank like a stone in his chest.

"And you, Grayson, are the reason this is all happening—"

"No, he is *not!*" Aunt Linda snapped.

"Yes, he is!" Jason's eyes burned. "Because thirteen years ago, they were done for good! And then along came Grayson. Spoiled, stupid Grayson. And Mom stuck it out for twelve more years with that sick jerk, just for you."

Tears oozed down Grayson's cheeks. His voice caught in his throat. For a moment, he forgot all about the Sulfurians. All he could do was let Jason's words sink in. He hoped, he prayed that Mason wasn't hearing Jason's tirade.

"Jason," Aunt Linda whispered. "Get out. Go home. I will deal with you later."

"He's not a little kid anymore," Jason's voice broke. "He needs to understand these things." He scowled, shook his head, and slammed the door on his way out.

The room spun. Grayson collapsed, but Aunt Linda caught him. He sobbed into her shoulder. "Shh, Grayson, please. He did *not* mean those things."

Grayson choked, "Yes, he did."

"I swear to you, he did *not*. He is just... very, very stressed and angry. He's angry about so much, and it wasn't fair for him to unleash all of that on you. Listen, Grayson. I am not happy about what happened out there—"

"I was trying to do the right thing, I—"

"—but I love you. Your brothers love you. Your parents love you."

She guided Grayson into the office chair and wiped

the tears from his eyes. "Okay," she sighed. "One thing at a time. It's the only way we can deal with a day like today, right?"

Grayson nodded.

"Jason is so angry right now. Because when he was younger, your parents' marriage was even tougher, okay? He saw things and heard things and felt their problems a lot more than you or Mason ever did."

"It's true, isn't it?" Grayson sniffled. "When I was born, it made them stay together. It made them unhappy."

"It's not true at all," Aunt Linda assured him. "Grayson, your parents were never happier than they were after you and Mason came along. Believe me. Nobody knows my sister like I do. She loves your dad. They love each other, but their relationship has always been tough. That's not your fault, or your brothers' faults. It's just between them.

"They worked through a lot. They were happy for a long time. It wasn't until recently that things got hard again."

"I know what Dad did," Grayson said. "I do. I get it. I'm not an idiot like Jason thinks I am. But why is it so wrong to believe he can change? That he can fix this?"

Aunt Linda opened her mouth to speak but couldn't find the words.

"Do you hate him?"

"He's..." Aunt Linda struggled. "He isn't my favorite person right now. But... I know he cares about your mom. I know he loves you boys more than anything. I respect that about him."

"Well, I love him," Grayson said. "And I love my brothers and my mom, and I hate that..."

"You hate that your brother hates your dad," Aunt

Linda said. "You wish you could change that." She brushed a tear off Grayson's check. "Maybe someday you will."

Grayson sighed.

"You know, Grayson, you and I are both middle children. It's like being a diplomat. That's why I've always excelled in hospitality and business. The middle child is the glue that holds the family together. Whether you like it or not, that will always be your job."

"Tell that to Jason," Grayson said.

"Well, Jason is right that you're at a point in your life where you need to step up and be accountable. But you're right that Jason hasn't been a good role model this summer. He's letting his anger control him."

Grayson glanced up. His heart pounded. "What did you just say?"

"I said that Jason's anger is getting the better of him. And you, Grayson, have always been such a cool guy. Cool guys build bridges, help people understand one another, figure out problems. Maybe Jason is right that sooner or later you'll have to get a *little* angry at your dad. That's healthy. But Jason needs to... cool off a little, I guess. You guys are having such a hard time with each other right now because..."

"Because we need each other," Grayson whispered.

Aunt Linda smiled.

Grayson's heart pounded. "Oh no..."

"What is it?"

Grayson stood. "It's Jason! I'm so sorry, Aunt Linda. I'm so, so sorry about everything that's going on, but I have to find him, now!"

"What? Why?"

"I'll explain later!" Grayson rushed toward the

door. *I am officially the worst brother ever!* he thought.

Aunt Linda called after him as he bolted through the kitchen toward the ballroom, weaving around the busy staff. "Pardon me, coming through! Emergency!" *All day, I've been worried sick about my younger brother, kept him safe in the Water Tower...*

He swiveled around a chef carrying a steaming hot kettle and rushed into the ballroom.

And all this time, the Sulfurians wanted my older brother!

Chapter 28

"Mason, come in!" Grayson splashed through puddles on the dance floor. There was no sign of Lucy or Sulfurians.

He examined the soaked head table. Still no trace of the Frost-Key.

"I'm here, Gray." Mason said. "What's going on? One minute you were shouting at Joanna, the next minute all I heard was Jason screaming."

A pit formed in Grayson's stomach. "How much of that did you hear?"

"Not much. Lucy cut in, and I had to mute your channel."

"I have good news, bad news, and ultra-horrible news," Grayson said.

"Okay," Mason said. "Give it to me in that order."

"Good news: The Sulfurian germ isn't inside Mr. Slynt. They only needed Slynt for the tower," Grayson said. "Bad news: I can't find the Frost-Key."

"Ultra-horrible?"

"I think the Sulfurian germ is inside our brother's head. That's why those drones approached me at Something Suite today. They didn't know I was the

Frost-Keeper until I stupidly revealed myself. They thought I was Jason."

"What!" Mason shouted. "Are you sure?"

"The germ feeds on human rage. Jason's been so angry about Dad for so long, and the germ has been making him even crazier. The things he said to me... I'm just glad you didn't hear it."

"Where's Jason now?"

"Aunt Linda sent him home, but some fire mage could have intercepted him." Grayson marched toward the lobby. "He could be—"

"What a mess you made, Frost-Keeper." Joanna stood, perfectly dry, with her hands folded in front of her. "Your big brother must be mortified."

"Grayson," Mason's voice interjected. "The GPS shows that Lucy is still in the hotel, but I can't raise her."

"How nice that baby brother is safely squirreled away. Sulfurians cannot hold the Frost-Key, but perhaps I could hypnotize a human pawn to fetch him and drag him into the impending fire."

"Don't threaten my brothers," Grayson said.

"Don't act like you have bargaining power, boy. You will go down in history as the ineptest Frost-Keeper to ever hold the key. Astounding that it chose you. Must be slim pickings in this digital age."

Mr. Cortez marched angrily in their direction. "What are you doing out here!"

Joanna flicked her palm and hypno-fire glided like a paper lantern past Cortez's eyes. "Be gone, fool."

Cortez's eyes went wide and blank. He immediately headed back into the lobby.

"We have your little girlfriend. We have big brother. And, most importantly, we have your key."

"Then what are you waiting for?" Grayson studied

her milky-white eyes. "Why don't you just incinerate me already?"

"The Grand Sulfurian has greater plans. Congratulations. You are not only the 102nd Frost-Keeper. You are also going to be the last one—ever." She headed into the lobby. Her voice echoed telepathically, *Follow me if you care about your loved ones. Don't do anything stupid.*

Grayson followed Joanna. Two male Sulfurian mages in shades linked arms with her and escorted her toward the elevators. Soaked party guests filled the lobby. Slynt's entourage and hotel management argued with the fire department.

Joanna approached the elevator, and Grayson noticed the shimmering silvery-copper panel on the floor. It finally dawned on him that the metal was adaptanium. It had changed from the Slynt Logo to a swirling fiery pattern. *Step onto the platform with us, Frost-Keeper,* came Joanna's voice.

Her Sulfurian escorts created swirling balls of hypno-fire that floated toward the lobby. In perfect unison, the entire crowd turned away from the elevators.

Grayson stepped onto the panel, and the platform descended underground. The adaptanium panel dipped beneath the floor, and a metal lid slid back over their heads, sealing them in a pitch-black tube.

Chapter 29

The Sulfurian mages removed their shades, casting an eerie orange glow against the adaptanium support beams of the elevator shaft.

"Clever," Grayson said. "There's an adaptatnium subbasement that only you Sulfurians can access. Your own private elevator."

"Good," Mason whispered in his ear. "Keep describing what's happening, Gray. It makes sense that the Sulfurians would have adaptanium tunnels, just like the Frost-Keeper."

"So, what do you fire freaks do down here?" Grayson asked as the elevator came to a stop. Adaptanium gates slid open into a chrome tunnel. "Have evil meetings? Host barbeques?"

"The Slynt Hotel is more than a building, Frost-Keeper," Joanna explained.

Grayson followed her and her minions down the tunnel.

"Adaptanium is rare, but it has become essential to our survival."

"Mine too," Grayson said. "Though you guys seem to have a lot more of it."

"The first Frost-Keeper stole and corrupted a small piece of adaptanium. He linked it to a dimension of infinite ice and cold. Since then, Sulfurians have struggled to spawn. But today, we reclaim our ancestral spawning grounds."

The chrome tunnel opened into a huge chamber, the size of the entire foundation of the hotel. A circle of adaptanium pillars stretched several stories to the top of a metal dome.

"Whoa," Grayson said. Then he added, for Mason's sake, "There is a huge stadium with giant adaptanium pillars and stuff under the hotel."

"You have a penchant for stating the obvious, Frost-Keeper." Scarlett Fury *prick-procked* into view. Her eyes blazed like miniature suns. Her mouth stretched into a circular O, and her skin peeled back. Her true Sulfurian form emerged, and she stretched her claws in satisfaction.

The other Sulfurians peeled away their human flesh. Fire billowed from their jack-o'-lantern mouths. Joanna's Sulfurian form had dark, black burn marks and deep gouges where her flaming eyes should be. But the fire in her mouth glowed whitish-blue.

"Blood-Wing and his waifs are in position, Joanna," Scarlett said. "His Grand Master is making final preparations for arrival, but he wishes to speak with the disarmed Frost-Keeper."

"Speaking of disarmed," Grayson said. "Could I like... see my Frost-Key? Just to, you know, say goodbye?"

"He is such a fool," Scarlett said to Joanna, ignoring Grayson.

"Agreed," Joanna said. "I'm almost disappointed by how easy this has been."

"Hey! I'm standing right here," Grayson muttered.

"Keep them talking," Mason said. "Buy time. Get me some intel."

"So, what exactly are you going to do with me now that you caught me?" Grayson asked. "I'm confused about your evil plan, to be honest."

"Patience, Frost-Keeper," Joanna said. "It is not for us to reveal your fate. His Volcanic Excellency will have the final word. Prepare to cower in his rage!"

Rage, Grayson thought. *Of course. Sulfurians are all about anger. They even hatch their stupid germ with negative human emotions.* "You know what?" Grayson said. "It's cool."

Scarlett Fury's eyes narrowed. "It's... what?"

"It's cool. I mean, sucks that you guys are going to burn the city to the ground just to hatch your germ. But I still have to give you credit. You Sulfurians bested me, the City of Chicago, the whole human race." Grayson smiled. "It's downright admirable."

Scarlett leaned closer. The heat from her face scorched Grayson's skin. Smoke billowed from her orifices. "You find it *admirable* that we will decimate your family, your home, and the legacy of the accursed Frost-Keepers?"

"Yes," Grayson said. "I'm *happy* for you." He beamed at Joanna and her two guards. "All of you. Really. Well done."

Joanna's jagged grin twisted into a scowl. "Are we certain this one is the Frost-Keeper? He is so completely inept."

"That is not a nice thing to say." Grayson shrugged and maintained his smile. He allowed a light, relaxed feeling to fill his chest. "But I forgive you. I suppose Sulfurians just don't understand people all that well."

"We have studied humans for centuries!" Blue fire swelled in Joanna's mouth. "We evolved *specifically* to manipulate and control you!"

Now's my chance, Grayson thought. *Get them super angry, then redirect that anger.* "Clearly, the waifs are the most highly evolved Sulfurians. What with the wings and all."

Scarlett scoffed. "Waifs are pathetic. Useful only in certain strategic scenarios. But what strategy could be implemented without a warrior's expertise?"

Smoke billowed from Joanna's human husk. Her two mages sneered with equal rage. "I seem to recall this boy slipping through the cracks of your *every* effort today, Scarlett Fury. It was *my* careful planning and manipulation that has delivered him to his Grand Master."

"Okay, ladies, settle down." Grayson held his hands out in a calming gesture. "Capturing me was a team effort. Everyone gets equal credit."

"Don't you dare take credit!" Scarlett's face erupted like a volcano. Grayson ducked out of the way as she lunged for Joanna. The assistant mages grappled with her.

Grayson darted across the dome, away from his distracted captors. "God, I hope my Frost-Key is down here somewhere!"

"The Sulfurians can't touch it," Mason said. "It's probably with a human they're controlling, Mr. Slynt or Cortez. Probably not Jason if he has the germ inside his head."

Grayson ducked behind an adaptanium pillar.

"You foolish mages let him slip away!" Scarlett's voice echoed. "You cannot escape us, Frost-Keeper!"

"This is not our fault!" Joanna shouted. "I will snuff you out like a candle, Fury."

"*Silence!*" A thunderous voice boomed.

A gargantuan ball of orange light exploded in the center of the dome, and a shockwave blasted Grayson against the wall. Waves of oppressive heat smothered over him as a vortex of fire swirled into an enormous yellow head with a bushy beard of atomic flame and thick, arched eyebrows.

"*Frost-Keeper!*" the voice bellowed. "You stand accused of centuries of crimes against the Sulfurian Empire! What have you to say for your legacy of disruption?"

"Well," Grayson struggled to his feet. "I guess I would say, in my defense, that it's my first day, and I'm still kinda new to all this stuff."

The gigantic head of the Grand Sulfurian roared. A wall of fire circled the dome. Grayson leapt out of its way, into the inner circle. Fire closed around him, forcing him toward the enormous angry head.

"We have long waited for the fall of the Frost-Keeper!" His gleaming mouth spread into an evil nuclear smile.

The shadows of Sulfurian drones appeared in the wall of fire. They marched toward Grayson, surrounded him.

"Gray!" Mason's voice came through static. "What's happening?"

"Mason," he said. "I love you, buddy. Stay where you are. Stay safe. Do you understand me?"

"Grayson?"

The Sulfurians converged on Grayson. He struggled, but they pinned his arms behind his back. They strapped a strange metal harness around his shoulders. The bands shimmered copper and silver. It looked like an adaptanium straight-jacket.

"This harness will subdue you forever, Frost-

Keeper," The Sulfurian said. "It is specially designed to force you into a state of cryogenesis."

"Cryogenesis?" Grayson struggled. "The thing where I sleep until I pass my powers on to the next Frost-Keeper? Why would you want that?"

"Because, by forcing you into an early slumber, you will never have time to hone your power. You will have no skill to pass on to the next Frost-Keeper. You see, boy, there has been an endless legacy of Frost-Keepers to plague our spawning ritual. If we simply incinerated you, as you undoubtedly deserve, sooner or later, the Frost-Key would seek out a new warrior.

"But by keeping you alive, in eternal frozen slumber, and keeping you apart from your weapon forever, you will simply blank out into unconsciousness. Never to reawaken. Never to pass on your legacy of frozen mischief."

Grayson's feet started to frost over. Ice crept up his arms and shoulders. His vision blurred white. "I... you can't..." He was suddenly too tired to speak. Too disoriented to think straight.

"Grayson! Stay awake!" his brother's voice echoed in his ear. "Please!"

The Grand Sulfurian's laughter rumbled. The chamber shook, and the adaptanium harness vibrated along with his cruel voice. "It is no use, boy. You will never awaken again. You will never die. You will never have peace. And you will live forever in a fretful sleep of wretched failure."

Grayson's heart sank. His eyelids dropped. He collapsed on the metal altar as ice enveloped his head. His mind completely whited out.

The last thing he heard was Mason calling his name, fading into distant nothingness.

Chapter 30

At first, Grayson only sensed pure white, like fresh snow in every direction.

Then a voice emerged from the blankness. "Heck of a first day, kid."

Grayson flexed his hands. His eyes adjusted as a human form took shape, white like the snow.

He examined his own body. His skin gleamed in the light of some invisible sun. He ran his hands up and down his chest. His body was pure translucent ice.

"Am I dead?"

"No," the other figure said. "Only sleeping."

"Victor?"

A bearded man, pure ice, like Grayson, approached, camouflaged in white. "Think of me as an echo that Victor left behind, Grayson. But I am here to help."

"Victor, I failed," Grayson said. "I'm sorry. The Frost-Key picked the wrong guy."

"You're the right guy, Grayson. And you haven't failed yet. There's usually a way out."

"Usually? I'm unarmed, frozen solid, and trapped

in a secret chamber, surrounded by Sulfurians. My brother Jason's brain is about to get roasted, and The Great Chicago Fire Part Two could be starting any minute." Grayson took a deep breath. "But if you have a suggestion to fix even *one* of those things, I'm all ears."

"You're in a better position than you realize, Grayson. If the Sulfurians understood the first thing about the Frost-Keeper's cryogenesis," Victor grinned, "they would never have put this plan into action."

"*I* don't understand the first thing about it," Grayson said.

"We are in a mental realm called the Frostscape. It's like a special dream, linked not just to you and me—and the collective psyches of every Frost-Keeper before us—but also to the tower and the key. Adaptanium can be used as a medium for communication."

"Those ice arrows!" Grayson shouted. "That was you?"

"It was all of us." Drake snapped his fingers. Out of the whiteness, more Frost-Keepers took shape, men and women with different styles of armor and unique icy weapons in their hands. Axes, swords, daggers, staffs. "We are the sum total of the collective experience of the Frost-Keepers, ever present in both the key and the Frostscape."

"All day long, every time I was in a jam, and I suddenly got some brilliant ice-power idea," Grayson said. "That was you guys, wasn't it?"

"The heroics were yours alone, Grayson," Victor said. The frozen forms faded behind him. "Our collective just provided some gut instinct and reflexes. And we guided you to the tower, of course.

Took you a while."

"You know," Grayson said. "Arrows are great, but ice letters, maybe some that spell out 'go to the Water Tower on Michigan Avenue,' would have been nice, too."

Victor smiled. "It's not exactly a precise science. I'll show you." Victor waved his arms, snow swirled into a portal that showed Mason pacing the Water Tower dome in a panic. Victor swirled another snowy portal that showed the Slynt penthouse where Joanna's two Sulfurian mages held Lucy hostage.

Mr. Slynt stood mesmerized at the side of the room. Grayson spotted the Frost-Key in his right hand.

"Lucy's dad has the key!"

"Yes, and while we can't tell Mason or Lucy what to do to help you in plain English, we can guide them," Victor explained. "For example, your brother saw the maps of my adaptanium tunnel system. A precise swirl of arctic wind, and a gentle line of frost on the right page of my journal could show him a safe route to the hotel."

"But my brother is safe in the Water Tower," Grayson said. "I ordered him to stay there."

"This is your choice, Grayson," Victor said. "But even if we can guide Lucy safely to the lobby, with the Frost-Key in hand, she doesn't know how to find you. Mason heard your description of the Sulfurian elevator."

Grayson wondered how he could feel so sick to his stomach in a mental realm. "If I don't send Mason to help me, everyone dies. But if I do send him and something happens to him... I... don't have a choice, do I?"

"The true choice is Mason's," Victor explained. "But unless we guide him, he won't know he has an option."

"I just yelled at Jason for not having faith in me," Grayson said.

Grayson watched Mason scanning the pages of Victor's journal.

"I guess I need to have a little faith in Mace." Grayson nodded. "Okay. What do I do?"

"Focus. Our thoughts connect to the ice and cold of the Water Tower, the connecting adaptanium chambers, and the Frost-Key itself. They won't respond to your thoughts as potently as if you were physically there, but in small, subtle ways you can manipulate the air." The portal zoomed in on Drake's journal. "Flip the pages, just a few dozen or so back should do it."

Grayson imagined a gust of cold air. The pages of the journal flicked backwards.

"Stop," Victor said.

Grayson calmed the wind. Mason pressed the new page flat to reveal a map of the lake, river, and tunnel system.

Victor Drake took Grayson's hand and guided it toward the surface of the portal. He traced Grayson's finger along one of the routes. "This path—" a frosty line crystallized on the surface of the page— "will connect your brother—" he guided the frost to the river entrance he and Lucy had found earlier— "to this pathway... to the train station."

He released Grayson's hand. Grayson traced the frosty line the rest of the way to the hotel.

"It is the safest way for Mason to travel. He will encounter no danger... until he arrives."

Mason's eyes grew wide. He shivered. "Grayson?"

"I'm here, Mace!" Grayson shouted.

"He cannot hear you, but he has an inkling you're

watching. Your connection to your brothers is strong, like your connection to the Frost-Key."

"Is there anything in the tower to protect my brother from Sulfurians?" Grayson asked.

"Nothing like the Frost-Key, I'm afraid," Victor said. "But I experimented with a heat-resistant adaptanium shield. You don't have to be a Frost-Keeper to wield it." Victor pulled the view out and pointed toward a round sheet of metal, mounted to the wall. "It's better than nothing."

Grayson focused. An arrow of ice cut across the floor and pointed toward the display. A second arrow crept up the wall and pointed directly at the shield.

Mason rushed across the room. He removed the shield and turned it over in his hands. "I should take this?" he asked.

Grayson desperately wanted to write the word *Yes* on the floor in ice. He concentrated, but all that came out was another line of ice that pointed toward the exit in the center of the room.

Mason strapped the adaptanium shield over his wrist and headed for the slick spiral staircase.

Then Mason hesitated. He rushed back to the desk and grabbed Victor's journal. He stuffed the book into an old leather carrying case and hurried down the stairs, struggling to keep his balance.

"Mason's path is at three o'clock," Victor explained. "Focus and open it. He does not require the key to access the system from inside the Water Tower."

Grayson concentrated and the brickwork slid open, revealing an icy tunnel. Mason entered the tunnel system, out of view of their portal.

"While Mason is in transit," Victor explained, "we have to help Lucy reclaim the Frost-Key. If she escapes to the lobby, Mason can guide her to you. The key's universal interface should be able to control the Sulfurian elevator."

Grayson studied the room. Lucy stewed in the corner, glaring at Joanna. Mr. Slynt stood stiff as a soldier, eyes blank.

Joanna loomed over Lucy. Hypnotic fire swirled over her palms. "If I could only wipe that defiance off your face, Lucienne Slynt. See how readily your father folds into submission?"

"Uh-oh," Grayson whispered.

Fiery patterns swirled between Joanna's fingertips.

Lucy grew calm.

"Yes!" Joanna smiled. "At last, you succumb to my power. All it took was time. Arise."

Lucy stood, her face blank like her father's. Then she spit right between Joanna's eyes.

Joanna growled and wiped her face. "Still, you resist me!"

"You can burn me to cinders, Joanna Crisp," Lucy snapped. "I will never be your slave."

"Oh, I plan to keep you and your father alive," she explained. "You see, the Slynt Tower is designed to withstand the coming inferno, and we need to keep it in Sulfurian hands for future spawnings."

"Grayson will stop you!"

"Your boyfriend is out of commission." Joanna snatched Lucy's face. Fire danced around her neck, orbited her head.

Sweat beaded on Lucy's forehead; she struggled to breathe.

"I am going to study your brain, Lucienne, and see what makes you so good at resisting my control. Sooner or later, like all pathetic humans, you will break." She shoved Lucy against her chair.

Lucy gasped for air.

"Don't forget, brat," Joanna hissed. "Even if I can't control you, even though I don't intend to kill you just yet, there's always that pretty face to scorch and scar."

"I hate that lady so much," Grayson growled.

"Hate won't get you through this," Victor said. "Anger, frustration, hatred. Those are the emotions that disrupt your powers."

"Like when Jason was yelling. When the pressure was on, I struggled to summon the Frost-Blade."

"Exactly. Stay cool. Stay focused," Victor said. "We're lucky that Lucy's will is so strong. Resisting hypno-fire is a rare talent."

"She's definitely stubborn." Grayson studied the room. He focused on the Frost-Key in Mr. Slynt's grip. "Her dad is stubborn too, though. If Lucy can resist, I'll bet he can too."

"Good thinking," Drake said. "Ever splashed your face with cold water, Grayson?"

"Yeah. When I'm tired, and I want to—Oh! We can use the key to jolt Slynt out of his hypno-daze!"

"Worth a shot," Victor said. "Remember: Sulfurians can't hold the Frost-Key. Even touching it gives them excruciating, mystical frostbite."

"But there are three mages in the room," Grayson said. "Even if I can summon a Frost-Blade for Lucy to fight with, I don't think she can take all three."

"She only needs to slay Joanna," Victor reminded him. "Without a head fire mage, the others are useless drones."

Joanna cackled. "Our Grand Leader's rebirth will blanket this city in an ocean of fire!"

Grayson concentrated. He sent a shiver of cold into the Frost-Key, up Alexander Slynt's hand. Slynt shook. His teeth chattered, and he dropped the Frost-Key. The key bounced across the floor and knocked into Joanna's heel.

Joanna shouted. A dark blue crust crept up her ankle, and she stumbled in pain.

Lucy dove for the key.

Her father shook his head in confusion. "What's going on? It's f-freezing in here!"

"Burn the girl!" Joanna snarled.

Lucy rushed to her father's side. She held the key toward the three Sulfurians.

Mr. Slynt's jaw dropped at the sight of the fiery-eyed mages. "Who are you people? Joanna! What is this?"

"Silence, you twit." Joanna stepped in front of them. "Drop the key, girl. You cannot summon its power! No one can now!"

"Guess again, witch." Grayson focused. A frosty hilt swirled around Lucy's fingers, and the Frost-Blade stabbed right through Joanna's heart. Her milk-white eyes widened with shock.

Ice crept over Joanna's human form. She struggled to speak as her jaw froze in place. The frozen skin of her human husk cracked, and she shattered. Blue orbs of fire pulsed in the air where she had stood. The fire faded and snuffed out.

Her two mages collapsed. Smoke poured from their eyes, and they writhed on the floor in pain.

Grayson cut a series of ice arrows across the Slynts' designer rug toward the exit. Lucy spotted them. She tugged her father's arm. *"Papa, dépêchez-vous! Suis moi!"*

The Slynts encountered two Sulfurian drones blocking the elevator. Lucy held out the Frost-Blade in front of her. Grayson transformed it into a shield to block a series of fireballs.

Lucy rushed the drones after their attack.

"Yikes, Lucy give me a sec!" Grayson swiftly sharpened her weapon back into a blade, and she sliced through both guards, rendering them into permafrost. Snow dusted her shoulders.

"Yes!" Grayson shouted. "I am so into that girl!"

"Really?" Victor said. "I hadn't noticed."

Lucy hastily attempted an explanation in French as she rode the elevator down with her father. Slynt shook his head in a daze. They emerged in the lobby just as Mason came huffing toward the adaptanium Slynt logo on the floor.

"Mason!" Lucy shouted. "I have the Frost-Key!" She hoisted the Frost-Blade, as if he could miss it.

A circular hole appeared in the center of the Slynt logo. Grayson focused. He made dozens of ice arrows all point to the adaptanium lock.

A horde of Sulfurians rushed into the lobby, hurling fireballs. Mason blocked the attacks with his adaptanium shield.

"Come on!" Grayson shouted. "Just stab the stupid seal!"

"There's some kind of elevator here, in the floor, I think," Mason shouted. "Use the key!"

Lucy jammed the Frost-Blade into the keyhole and the floor dropped down. Fireballs sailed over their heads as Lucy, Mason, and Mr. Slynt descended into the Sulfurian subbasement.

Grayson's heart quickened with panic. "There's bound to be Sulfurians guarding me."

He felt Victor's hand on his shoulder. "Have faith."

"Lucy, what is this place?" Mr. Slynt asked. "What were you saying about Joanna?" Still dazed, he followed Mason and Lucy down the chrome tunnel.

"It's what I have been trying to tell you since I arrived, Papa," Lucy said. "Joanna is a demon-witch from a dimension of infinite fire trying to destroy us all."

"I..." Understanding washed over Slynt's face. "I just thought all kids hated their future stepmothers."

"Joanna isn't anyone's future anything." Lucy smiled. "Not anymore. We have to find Grayson North. He's the only one who can save us."

"That no good, river-diving punk?"

"My brother is not a punk!" Mason snapped. "He's a hero!"

Grayson smiled.

They entered the enormous adaptanium chamber. The fiery face of the Grand Sulfurian was gone, but Grayson's body remained, frozen solid in the center of the room. Five Sulfurian guards surrounded him. One by one, their mouths and eyes blazed alert.

"This couldn't just be easy." Grayson expanded Lucy's Frost-Blade into a shield, big enough to protect her and her father. Mason backed behind them and held his own shield up as fireballs exploded over their heads.

"How are they supposed to get close enough to free me?" Grayson asked.

"The Frost-Key is less than ten yards from your physical body," Victor said. "Concentrate, Grayson. The closer the proximity, the stronger your connection to the key."

Grayson focused. Arctic wind rushed through the chamber. A wall of ice sprouted between the Sulfurian guards and Grayson's rescue crew. Lucy's shield narrowed back into a sword.

"How are you doing that, Lucy?" Mason asked. "I thought only the Frost-Keeper could—"

"It's not me." She smiled. "It's Grayson. I can feel him, guiding us."

"You got that right!" Grayson shouted. "Now let's finish this." Icy stalagmites erupted beneath the five Sulfurian drones. Each of them exploded into frost.

Grayson cheered. "Take that, you hot-blooded anger-management rejects!" He turned to the icy echo of Victor Drake. "Not bad for my first day, huh?"

"You can learn a lot in one day." Victor smiled. "But it's not over yet, Grayson."

Mason and Lucy hurried to Grayson's frozen form. The Frost-Blade melted, revealing the key, and a keyhole appeared on Grayson's adaptanium harness.

"Victor," Grayson said. "Thank you for helping me. What else do I need to know? How do I stop the Sulfurians for good? How do I save Jason?"

Victor Drake shook Grayson's frozen hand. "There's nothing more I need to teach you, Grayson North." He faded into wintery-white. "You're ready."

Shadows swallowed the white realm. Grayson's eyes popped open. Every muscle in his body convulsed, and the metal harness popped off. He found himself back in the Sulfurian chamber.

Lucy and Mason hugged him. Slynt stood dumbfounded behind them, still glancing around in disbelief at the enormous chamber.

Grayson stood and stretched. "I love you guys! Thank you so much!"

He kicked the adaptanium harness and accepted the Frost-Key from Lucy. It cooled his palm. Refreshing, invigorating cold swirled into his limbs. "I will *never* let you go again," he kissed the tip of the Frost-Key. "I'm sleeping with this thing frozen to my hand for the rest of my life!"

"Your life is over, Frost-Keeper!" A burst of fire

marked Scarlett Fury's appearance, blocking the exit. "Glad to find you awake. This spawning was growing dull."

"Behind me!" Grayson stepped forward. Armor froze over his torso. Arctic energy surged through his body, and the Frost-Blade sharpened.

"A shame the harness failed." Scarlett's human face melted back. Her matchstick head blazed. "But now you'll die in battle!"

Chapter 31

Scarlett Fury's claws made neon streaks as she slashed toward Grayson. He pivoted and slicked the ground as her foot came down. Scarlett stumbled, and he dove for her ankles, freezing her feet to the floor.

Grayson rolled to safety, constructed an ice shield, and deflected a second strike. Scarlett's torso rotated 360 degrees; her claws melted streaks in Grayson's shield.

Grayson reinforced his armor with another layer of spikes and frosted padding.

"Pathetic!" Scarlett's face blazed like a star. The ice around her feet puddled and steamed. "Whatever trickery you used to escape cryogenesis will not save you in battle, Frost-Keeper!"

Grayson slashed. White-hot claws intercepted the Frost-Blade. She burned hotter. Grayson's armor started melting. Water dripped down his face.

"Your blade is deadly to Sulfurian flesh, but it is not indestructible." Scarlett's mouth pulsed nuclear white.

Grayson strained against her searing hot fingers.

"Ice is ice! Cold is cold," Scarlett snarled. "But my will is an inferno!"

Grayson channeled all his energy into the frozen blade. The edges started to melt against the blazing daggers of Scarlett's fingertips.

"Your brother's essence will burn away forever in the rebirth of our Great Leader!" Her talons finally melted through the Frost-Blade and sent chucks of ice flying in every direction.

Grayson leapt away, just barely avoiding her magma claws. He aimed the hilt of his broken sword, and summoned an explosion of ice spikes between them. *Don't lose your cool,* Grayson reminded himself. *That's exactly what she wants.*

Scarlett's warrior minions gathered behind Grayson. He spun, grew a newer, sharper Frost-Blade, and sliced through two of their necks. The heads and torsos burst into permafrost. A third minion hesitated and Grayson impaled it on a giant spike.

He twisted around in time to deflect an ambush from Scarlett. Her claws sparked against the Frost-Blade.

Grayson hacked and slashed, but Scarlett skillfully blocked each strike. She howled with rage, swiped, and broke the icy blade a second time.

Grayson immediately grew another Frost-Blade and smiled. "I get it now."

"You understand nothing!" She snarled and slashed.

He continued to counter her attacks. "You Sulfurians use anger against people. But I'm not falling for it anymore. The more I keep my cool, the more in tune I am with the Frost-Key, the more powerful I become."

Scarlett Fury screamed. Pillars of fire spewed from her face and hands. Grayson flipped toward the center of the adaptanium altar.

"Ignorant whelp!" She raised her claws. A fiery sphere glowed and expanded over her head. "Nothing can save you or your world!"

"Grayson, look out!" Mason shouted from across the dome.

Grayson slid aside, just as Scarlett hurled her massive fire-ball at the center of the sphere. He braced himself for an explosion, but instead the glob of fire simply melted into the adaptanium floor.

The pattern in the center of the dome glowed. Neon orange and yellow patterns illuminated across the altar, up the lines of the adaptanium pillars, all the way to the ceiling. The patterns at the top of the dome lit like hot coals.

"All is lost now and forever, Frost-Keeper." Scarlett laughed. "It does not matter that you slayed our fire mage. It does not matter even if you best me in battle. The Slynt Hotel has already begun to channel the energy of our dimension. Your brother waits on the roof, burning with rage, waiting to be consumed!"

Grayson shook with anger. He desperately tried to calm himself. His armor started to crack.

"Gray! Don't listen to her!" Mason shouted. "It's not over! There's still time!"

"Silence, brat!" Scarlett Fury flicked her claws. Fireballs rocketed over Grayson's shoulders, toward his brother.

Grayson fired an arctic white pulse and disintegrated the blasts before they could reach Mason and the Slynts. He carved a line with his Frost-Blade and a protective Ice-Wall formed to shelter his allies.

He turned to face Scarlett, only to find the scorching oven of her face inches from his eyes. Grayson shouted in pain and fell backwards. He struggled to maintain his frozen armor.

Scarlett slashed down. He rolled away in time, but she sliced the tip of his Frost-Blade again. He regrew it and jabbed at her, but Scarlett's Sulfurian torso wormed out of reach.

She pinned his wrists with her white-hot claws. Her face spewed fire over him.

Grayson screamed. He gripped his Frost-Key, struggled to keep an icy coating over his body, but the heat of Scarlett's inferno was evaporating his armor as quickly as he could generate it.

"Die, Frost-Keeper!"

Suddenly, a loud *clang!* reverberated. The fire died down.

Alexander Slynt bashed Scarlett Fury in the face with Mason's adaptanium shield a second time, and she staggered backwards. Her eyes sputtered fiery stars. Slynt hit her again. And again. "Get!" *Clang!* "Out!" *Clang!* "Of my!" *Clang!* "Hotel!"

Slynt hoisted the shield for one last bash. "And stay away from my daughter's date!"

Scarlett swiped the shield out of his hands. Slynt tripped onto his back and banged his head against the metal floor.

Scarlett's claws flexed. "Your usefulness has ended, rich man!" She slashed down.

Grayson summoned arctic wind to throw her off balance, and her claws grazed the floor next to Slynt's head. He aimed his Frost-Blade and fired an ice blast that pinned her ankles to the floor again.

Before Scarlett could melt herself free, Grayson leapt to his feet and poured a steady stream of ice around her legs. A frozen shell crept up Scarlett's body. Dense layers of ice thickened over her.

Scarlett burned hotter and hotter, but she couldn't break free. A cloud of steam billowed to the top of the luminescent dome.

"You Sulfurians are about to learn a hard lesson." Grayson sharpened his Frost-Blade. He advanced on Scarlett.

Two more of her minions rushed out of the shadows, but without so much as a glance, Grayson summoned ice-pillars from the floor that winterized and obliterated them.

"Brothers. Fathers. Daughters. Rich or poor. We're all the same," Grayson said. "And we don't go down without a fight. Don't mess with humans!"

"It is useless!" Scarlett's eyes spewed daggers of fire. "You will all burn!"

"Tough talk..." Grayson impaled the Frost-Blade into the icy cocoon, through Scarlett's heart. Her eyes and mouth went black. Her skin crusted with ice. "...for a popsicle."

Scarlett crumbled into ice and snow.

Chapter 32

"Thanks for the assist, Mr. Slynt." Grayson helped Mr. Slynt to his feet as Lucy and Mason rounded the protective frozen barrier.

"I would love to know everything that's been going on down here in this glowing temple of doom," Slynt said. "But there have been more than a few misunderstandings today. And, um... I'm sorry I called you..."

"A no-good punk, a river rat, a hoodlum, a—"

"Yes, yes, all of that." Slynt nodded and locked eyes with Grayson. He placed a hand on his shoulder. "Thank you for protecting my daughter." Slynt immediately pulled his hand away and wiped it on his jacket. "Your shoulder is freezing."

"Papa!" Lucy hugged her father. "Are you okay?"

"I am, Lucy." He hugged her back. "Thanks to you."

Lucy provided her father with more explanation. Much of it was in French, but Grayson caught the words "Sulfurian," "Frost-Keeper," and "Chicago Water Tower."

Grayson studied the glowing adaptanium patterns of the pillars and dome. "Mace, do you have any idea how we can stop this thing?"

Mason produced Victor's journal from his bag. "The Sulfurians are opening a portal to bathe the human host... Jason... in heat from their dimension." He flipped to the section about the spawning. "The process takes time. Blood-Wing and their remaining forces must be guarding Jason on the roof. The rift is temporary. Eventually, it closes on its own."

"But if we don't save Jason, that won't matter." Grayson closed Victor's journal and pushed it back into his brother's leather bag. "Mason, I'll need you to talk me through this."

Mason nodded.

"Follow me, everyone. Watch out for flame brains." Grayson led the group out the chrome tunnel to the Sulfurian elevator. Dark shadows swallowed them up as they ascended the adaptanium shaft, but a strange hum persisted, as if the entire hotel were vibrating with energy.

"My security must already be working to evacuate the hotel and assess the situation," Slynt said. "I'll make sure everyone gets to a safe distance. I'll find your aunt as well."

"I'm not sure if there is a safe distance." The Frost-Key glinted in Grayson's hand. "The only place I know for sure that's safe is the Water Tower... but you need the key to get in."

"There's no time for you to take us there," Lucy said. "You have to help Jason."

The circular panel slid open, and light from the lobby washed over them.

"Everyone is counting on me." Grayson's voice shook. "Even Victor couldn't thwart the last spawning without consequences, and he's twice the Frost-Keeper that I—"

"Grayson North!" Lucy shot him her *look*. Then she took his hand and squeezed his fingers around the Frost-Key. "You *can* do this."

"I hope so."

She smiled. "I know so."

Grayson's breath steamed as they rose into the lobby. Guests were already evacuating. A few stopped to stare in disbelief at the ice-covered kid and his crew emerging from a secret panel. But the onlookers were quickly ushered along by security.

"Get my brother someplace safe!" Grayson told Slynt. "I'm heading for the roof." He tapped his earpiece. "I'll be right here, Mace!"

Grayson rushed through the crowd. "Pardon me! Freeze-dried superhero heading to a situation! One side please!"

The crowd collectively gasped and murmured.

"Not one of them! Good guy here! I know my face is a little frosty, but I promise, underneath I'm really cool."

Strobes of fire flashed outside the glass doors of the lobby. Explosions echoed. The crowd screamed with panic.

"Everyone, please!" Grayson shouted. "Follow the authorities' instructions, evacuate in an orderly fashion, and—if I could just ask for one small favor— I need a runway here." He gestured toward the door.

The crowd calmed and parted in stunned amazement.

"Perfect. Thanks!" Grayson got a running start and leapt onto an ice-slick. He shot toward the lobby doors.

People screamed and cheered as Grayson froze, shattered, and slid right through the glass doors.

Outside, streaks of fire danced across the

darkening sky. Heavy clouds had rolled in over the lake, and the shadows of winged waifs wove in and out of the gray sky.

Crowds gathered across the river. Sirens blared. The people evacuating the hotel pointed and shouted, in shock and amazement, at Grayson. He gave a friendly wave, and the crowd cheered.

That's more like it! Grayson thought. *Finally, without all the dumb hypno-fire, people are as amazed as they should be!*

The sun was setting over the skyline past the western fork of the Chicago River. A strange, warped energy, like hot air over concrete undulated up the side of the Slynt building. The adaptanium infrastructure was channeling energy from the foundation toward the roof—toward Jason.

"Are you happy, Frost-Keeper!" A tall, dark-haired man ascended the concrete steps from the Riverwalk. His eyes blazed like fire. "Now your fellow humans can truly appreciate the horrors of the spawning."

Grayson recognized the voice. "Impressive, Blood-Wing. You're even uglier as a human."

Blood-Wing sneered. "You bested Joanna and Scarlett Fury."

Grayson shrugged. "I had help."

"You are the first Frost-Keeper in centuries to slay the Head Fire Mage and expose us to a population."

"And don't forget, this is the 21st Century!" Grayson boasted. "So we're talking instant global coverage! You guys just went viral."

"Indeed, congratulations are in order." Blood-Wing gave a slow clap. "Joanna and Scarlett underestimated you, but I will not repeat their error."

"So are we going to fight or what?" Grayson's Frost-

Blade stabbed into place.

"Most certainly." Blood-Wing laughed. "After all there's still plenty of time to defeat me, charge the rooftop, overwhelm a horde of my most cunning waifs. And who knows, perhaps even reach dear brother." Blood-Wing snapped his fingers.

Leathery wings flapped. Two pumpkin-faced waifs rose behind Blood-Wing, each holding the arm of a hostage.

The waifs tilted the woman's head back revealing an unconscious Aunt Linda.

"But do you have time to save your Auntie?" Blood-Wing's human skin ripped apart into two enormous wings. His torso erupted like a Roman candle. "Let's find out!"

Chapter 33

Grayson formed an ice-slick and sped toward Blood-Wing and his waifs.

Blood-Wing beat his wings, Grayson swerved around licks of fire. He slashed at Blood-Wing, but the Sulfurian pivoted and rocketed into the sky.

The two waifs followed their boss, soaring out of reach. Grayson's fingertips brushed Aunt Linda's shoes as they carried her off. His enemies careened up the curved edge of the Slynt Hotel.

Grayson intensified his ice blast and sped after them. His ice-slick curled up the building's exterior, and Grayson boosted his speed up the wall. He added an updraft of arctic air for propulsion. His momentum pushed him on an icy trail that hugged the wall.

He kept his eyes on the three waifs, climbing higher.

This is the craziest thing I've done all day! Grayson's heart pounded with a mixture of terror and exhilaration. *But it's also the coolest.*

Grayson's ice-slick went completely vertical, only his speed and the stream of arctic wind held him in place. Waves of hot air pulsed along the concrete as the energy surged to the top.

The silhouettes of Blood-Wing and the two waifs holding Aunt Linda neared the roof. Grayson rushed past the roof deck pool area. His ice-slick shredded a beach umbrella.

He was more than halfway to the top.

Suddenly, scores of Sulfurian waifs poured over the edge of the roof. Wings flapped like thunder. Streams of fire blasted from their faces as they plummeted toward Grayson. Blood-Wing and Aunt Linda disappeared behind the incoming crowd.

Grayson increased his speed and swerved to dodge a storm of fireballs. He lashed out at the first line of waifs, slashing two into oblivion, still managing to keep his upward momentum. But from the corner of his eye, he spotted a waif swooping away with Aunt Linda.

Grayson tried to change direction and follow, but he lost momentum. His ice-slick faltered and his armor skidded against the glass windows of the skyscraper.

A waif tackled him. He stabbed and disintegrated it, but he had lost contact with the wall.

Grayson fell. He stretched his fingertips toward the pool deck. Pool water swirled and froze in his direction, but another waif battered him from the side, knocking him away from the pool.

Grayson froze himself to the waif. He intensified his armor to shield himself from the Sulfurian's fiery breath.

The waif snarled in surprise. The extra weight threw them even more off course, but the waif desperately beat its wings to slow their decent. They spiraled downward. Grayson summoned a powerful burst of winter air to push them closer to the river.

More waifs descended, like a murder of giant fiery crows. Once Grayson was sure they were over water, he stabbed the waif he had frozen himself to. His enemy burst into frost.

Grayson bulleted down, below the rest of the pack. He thickened his armor, braced for impact. Flames crisscrossed past him, until he finally hit the rippling surface of the Chicago River.

Grayson plummeted deep down. He glanced up and spotted glowing shapes. Fiery lines cut over the surface. He aimed his body downstream, stuck his Frost-Blade behind him and propelled himself like a frozen torpedo, toward the State Street Bridge.

Grayson surfaced and took a deep breath. Waifs were blasting the water where Grayson had fallen. Steam filled the air. The fiery shadows of winged Sulfurians swirled in and out of clouds wafting over the lake. It looked like a living nightmare, but the steam was giving him cover.

One of these guys still has Aunt Linda. Grayson scanned the clouds. He guessed, he hoped, the waifs were keeping her alive as a bargaining chip, using her to keep Grayson's focus away from Jason.

Above the steaming river, more waifs circled the hotel. Ribbons of heat crawled up the glass and pooled in the sky above the roof. Cries of frightened civilians filled the air. Traffic horns and sirens blared.

People must think it's the end of the world, Grayson realized. *The authorities need to understand what's going on to help contain the panic.*

Grayson propelled himself to the edge of the river and climbed onto the concrete. He rushed through steamy air, up the steps to street level, and scoured the sky for Aunt Linda.

"I have visibility on some strange stuff," came a familiar voice. "But there's a weird fog over the river. There was a white streak climbing the side of the Slynt Tower, and these... winged creatures swarmed it.... Look, we need to divert all traffic away from the riverfront."

Grayson made his way up to the bridge. He spotted Officer Lucas on his radio.

"Officer Lucas," Grayson said. "Could I have a word?"

The officer's eyes widened at the sight of the armored Frost-Keeper. He clicked his radio. "Give me a minute. I may have something for you."

"Tell the cops to keep civilians far away from the Slynt Hotel," Grayson said. "I need room to work."

"How do we take those things down? What is going on? Who the heck are you? And why... wait a second. Say something else." Officer Lucas squinted at him.

"It's a long story, all I can say is—"

"Wait a minute. Grayson?" Officer Lucas stepped closer. His eyes grew wide. "You're Chef Linda's nephew!"

"Shh! Not so loud!" Grayson put a finger over his frozen lips. "I'd like some semblance of a secret identity if I survive this."

"That crazy fire lady in the Red Line tunnel—"

"Was real, yep. Short version: they're interdimensional arsonists called Sulfurians."

"What are they doing at the hotel?"

"They're trying to respawn their leader, and if they succeed, it's Great Chicago Fire Part 2." Grayson held up his Frost-Blade. "This is the only weapon that can kill them, so save your ammo and focus on keeping people safe. But I need a favor."

"Name it."

"Get the Fire Department stationed along the bridges and riverfront. They are the ones we need on the front line in case I fail. Their hoses can't snuff out a Sulfurian, but they *can* create a perimeter and help keep all this fire contained."

"You got it. But Grayson, this is extremely dangerous. I don't think—"

A blazing Sulfurian waif dropped out of the steamy air. He spotted Grayson and blasted fire in their direction. Grayson erected an icy wall to block the attack, then fired an arctic beam that cut right through the Sulfurian. The waif burst into snow.

"I don't think you're... qualified to..." Officer Lucas shook his head in disbelief.

"Not up for debate! I appreciate the assist." More leathery wings sounded in the steam. "They're only after me. Lay low!" Grayson crafted an ice-chute to the river.

As he slid away, he heard Officer Lucas on his radio: "Patch me through to the fire chief."

Fire roared over Grayson's head. A Sulfurian tackled him from behind and shoved him into the water. Grayson splashed and grappled with the waif. He stabbed it into frost as more fireballs burst through the steam.

Grayson generated an ice floe to stand on just as three more waifs dropped from the cloudy canopy. Grayson stabbed the first two, dodged the snapping oven of the third's jaws, and impaled it through the heart.

Then he ice-surfed back toward the hotel. More angry waifs dropped down. He hacked and slashed his way past them, severing arms, slicing wings apart, and dodging fireballs. One by one he exploded his foes into snow.

"I am done messing around with you nuclear nutcakes!" Grayson shouted.

Another wave of waifs dove after him unleashing streaks of fire. Grayson stabbed his sword into the water. A wall of ice spikes fired up, impaling all of them, bursting them into white powder. "Bring me my aunt! Let my brother go! Leave my city, and never come back!"

Grayson channeled all his energy into the Frost-Blade. Arctic wind churned downriver, sweeping all the steam away and revealing the army of waifs above him.

The entire surface of the river hardened to ice. Frozen pillars shot into the air and exploded into spikes, like gigantic medieval maces. Jagged, wintery spires impaled and disintegrated dozens of waifs.

The remaining waifs circled and retreated higher into the air. An orange shape streaked over the water like a meteor. Blood-Wing flared his wings, slowed, and landed on the ice. His feet left a trail of steam as he approached Grayson.

A sword of pure fire sprouted between Blood-Wing's claws.

Chapter 34

"You have my attention, Frost-Keeper," Blood-Wing growled. "Truly, you have improved since this morning."

"You can learn a lot in one day." Grayson pointed the Frost-Blade at Blood-Wing. "Bring me my aunt, unharmed, or I will slay every last one of you chicken-winged, carbon clowns!"

Blood-Wing held up a hand, and the swarm of waifs above them parted. The two waifs from before carried Aunt Linda overhead. "Best me in battle." Blood-Wing's sword intensified into a pillar of white fire. "And I will *consider* letting her go."

"Gently set her down *safely* in a *safe* place!" Grayson clarified. "*Not* the dangerous kind of letting go. Let's be very clear about that."

Blood-Wing rolled his blazing-yellow eyes. "Very well. Prepare to die!" Blood-Wing spread his wings and charged.

They clashed. More steam spewed as the Frost-Blade locked against Blood-Wing's flaming sword. Grayson held his ground. He froze his feet to the surface of the river and channeled all his energy into the Frost-Blade.

"You think that sparkler is any match for the Frost-Blade?" Grayson laughed. "You're up against the battle-hardened instincts of a hundred-plus Frost-Keepers, magma mouth!"

"Is that anger I sense, Frost-Keeper?" Blood-Wing spun and they clashed blades again. Sparks and icicles exploded.

"I don't care if I have to deep freeze every last one of you ugly matchsticks; I will save my family and this city!"

Blood-Wing beat his wings. A vortex of fire circled them. They clashed swords again. "Even if you save your aunt, you have but precious minutes left before our Grand Leader spawns!" He pivoted and slashed. Tongues of fire rained from his wings.

Grayson let the Frost-Blade guide his movements. He blocked each swipe of Blood-Wing's blade and swirled arctic air to keep the heat at bay. Blood-Wing pivoted again. Transferring the sword to his right hand, Grayson ducked as Blood-Wing's left hand slashed upward. He hacked the tips of the Sulfurian's claws clean off.

Blood-Wing snarled, winced with pain, then in a flash of yellow flames, he retreated to the air. He sucked on his broken claws like a wounded animal, then he pointed with his sword. "Rend him to pieces!" His minions dove.

Grayson summoned icy spikes to skewer more of Blood-Wing's waifs. "I thought this was a one-on-one duel!"

"I never said that!" Blood-Wing snapped.

"It was heavily implied!"

More waifs maneuvered around the icy projectiles. Grayson was running out of space.

Suddenly, blasts of high pressure water knocked the descending waifs off course. Grayson glanced up. Lines of firetrucks flanked the river at street level. Firefighters sprayed their hoses over the river, battering the waifs.

"No!" Blood-Wing lunged; he hoisted his fiery weapon. Grayson focused on the jets of water and twisted them into icy tendrils. The ice swirled around Blood-Wing, ensnared him. Grayson tightened the icy trap and froze Blood-Wing between three of the jagged pillars he had created.

Blood-Wing snarled. The arm that held his fire-blade was frozen stiff. "Free me, you imbeciles!"

Grayson raised himself into the air on an icy column. As Blood-Wing's waifs sought to melt their commander free, Grayson blasted them into frost. Those he missed, the Fire Department knocked away with high-pressure jets.

Once again, Grayson harnessed the jets of water. He warped the hose spray into icy daggers that cut through the remaining waifs. Swirling blades of ice shredded through the horde, kept them away from the imprisoned Blood-Wing.

One by one, waifs burst into snow that sprinkled over the frozen river.

As his army diminished, Blood-Wing's eyes widened. Grayson rose higher on his pillar and cut an ice bridge to the captured Waif Commander. He slid toward him with the Frost-Blade poised for attack.

Blood-Wing's eyes narrowed into yellow knives. He shouted: "Drop the woman!"

Grayson spotted the stray waif to the left. He skewered Blood-Wing. The Sulfurian's face snuffed into black coal and frosted over.

As Blood-Wing's husk exploded into snow, Grayson slid past. He let himself plummet toward the water between the networks of icy structures. He increased his speed before making an ice ramp.

Aunt Linda was already falling to his left. Grayson launched himself in her direction. He summoned a blast of arctic wind to push him toward her.

Time seemed to slow. Fireballs pulsed between them. Drops of water sprayed in every direction. Finally, Grayson connected with Aunt Linda and supported her back. He pulled the firefighters' streams toward them, curved an icy chute beneath them and slid toward the State Street Bridge.

The firefighters must have caught on, because they were now aiming their hoses right at them. Grayson froze their streams, broadened the slide and created a slick ramp to hoist them over the edge of the bridge.

Time sped up. Grayson and Aunt Linda swerved inside the ice chute. They rocketed and tilted like human bobsleds. They slid over abandoned cars, toward street level.

Grayson's head throbbed. The level of concentration it had taken to pull her out of midair had left him totally exhausted, but his ice powers were still working their magic.

Ice poured over the bridge, devoid of focus or direction. Grayson's runaway ice-slick sent them spinning in different directions.

"No!" Grayson watched in horror as his aunt slid toward the opposite edge of the bridge. He struggled to get back to his feet and slipped.

Officer Lucas dove for Aunt Linda. He hooked his arms around her waist and stopped her from going over the edge. Then he pulled her to safety, away from the edge, and helped her down from the ice.

Aunt Linda groaned. "What's g-going on?" She shivered. "Why am I f-f-freezing?"

Grayson regained his composure and raced over to them. A fireball exploded between them. Grayson turned and slashed the head clean off one of the remaining waifs. Three more descended on the bridge, and Grayson skewered and obliterated each one.

The few remaining waifs started to retreat back to Slynt Tower.

Grayson gave a thumbs up to the firefighters across the river. They cheered and returned it.

Officer Lucas had pulled Aunt Linda behind his squad car for cover. He was asking her questions and checking her for injuries.

"Aunt Linda!" Grayson hurried over to them. He iced down, revealing his human face. "Are you okay?"

"She's fine," Officer Lucas assured him. "A couple scrapes, but she'll be okay."

"What's going on? Where are your brothers?" Aunt Linda grabbed his wrist and gasped. "Oh my God, you're frozen solid!"

"I'm okay. Mason's okay." Grayson's heart hammered. "But I need to save Jason. He's on the roof of the Slynt."

Aunt Linda's eyes widened at the Frost-Blade. "You need to bring me up to speed here, Gray."

"Aunt Linda, this is Officer Lucas. He's a huge fan. Officer Lucas, please bring my attractive and successful, and totally single aunt up to speed." He trained his eyes on the hotel. "I promise. We'll talk later."

Grayson made an ice ramp and glided toward Slynt Tower.

Chapter 35

Darkness loomed as the sun sank behind the skyline. A yellow aura glowed brighter around the Slynt Hotel. Grayson jetted faster upriver.

Suddenly, a huge shockwave pulsed from the top of the tower. An intense force nearly knocked Grayson off his ice-slick. A wide, orange circle swelled in the sky over the hotel.

The portal blazed brighter than the sun. It expanded until the sky glowed crimson daylight.

"No!" Grayson sped up. He warped the surface of the river into an ice-ramp and blasted back up the curved edge of the building. He accelerated up the wall, past the pool, even faster than before. Pushing himself with as much arctic wind and frozen propulsion as he could summon.

The fiery circle in the sky brightened. Bushy orange licks of flame sprouted, framing white-hot eyes. A huge orange beard poured into the air.

It's him, Grayson realized. *The Grand Sulfurian is here for real this time! Not just a projection.*

Grayson's ice slick rocketed faster. He neared the top, launched himself into the air, and landed on the roof. The enormous fiery face smoldered about fifty feet above the building. The Grand Sulfurian's laughter echoed across the cityscape.

Grayson spotted his brother on an adaptanium panel at the center of the roof. "Jason!" Dozens of Sulfurian warriors and waifs surrounded him. They immediately rushed Grayson.

Grayson hacked, stabbed, and slashed his attackers. He skewered them with ice spikes and pillars, and took out the stragglers with arctic beams. One by one they exploded into frost and snow.

"Jason! It's me! It's your brother! Listen to me!"

Jason's eyes glowed like a Sulfurian's. Heat billowed from the adaptanium panel at his feet, as well as down from the portal above, enveloping Jason in crimson light.

Grayson furiously bisected one horrible matchstick monster after the next. He fired ice beams that vaporized the airborne waifs. But after each attack, the intense heat from the Grand Sulfurian immediately melted and evaporated all the ice he could generate. Only his Frost-Blade and ice armor withstood the inferno.

"Gray, we're safe!" Mason's voice finally cut in. "But we can't find Aunt Linda!"

"Aunt Linda is okay," Grayson said. "I'm on the roof, Mace." Grayson stabbed another Sulfurian. "Jason is here. But I don't know if it's too late! I don't think he can hear me."

The Grand Sulfurian's voice boomed. "He cannot hear you, Frost-Keeper! He is an empty vessel. His mind has been burned away by glorious rage!"

"Don't listen to him!" Mason shouted. "It's not over until it's over. Get closer. Jason needs to hear your voice."

Grayson hacked and stabbed his way across the roof until only a handful of Sulfurian drones remained. Two remaining waifs swooped and snatched Grayson's arms. They attempted to drag him back over the edge, but Grayson's armor expanded with frozen spines and impaled them. Their frosty residue evaporated under the heat of the portal.

Grayson skewered the final few drones, and at last, cleared a path to Jason. Grayson thickened his armor as the Grand Sulfurian's face burned even hotter. Cold energy flowed from his Frost-Blade.

Fire and heat poured out of Jason. Grayson fought through a storm of flames, pushed toward his brother. Jason's face burned with a horrible grimace. His eyes were locked in an intense, angry stare of pure white light, just like the Grand Sulfurian's.

"Jace!" Grayson shouted. "It's me! It's your little brother, Jason. And I need you!"

Jason's stare remained locked in a furious inferno.

"I know you're mad," Grayson said. "About a lot of things. And I'm mad too."

Jason's eyes blazed hotter.

"Pathetic child! He cannot hear you!" the Grand Sulfurian bellowed.

Grayson kept shouting. "Jason! We need you now more than ever!"

"It is useless, Frost-Keeper!" Fiery spittle splattered down onto the Slynt roof as the Grand Sulfurian shouted.

Grayson extinguished flames with his Frost-Blade and advanced closer to his brother. "Jace, do you remember when Dad had to work, and you surprised me and showed up at the father-son hockey game?"

The Grand Sulfurian roared. More fire streamed

down from his mouth. Grayson cleared a path through it and kept powering through, closer to his brother.

"And afterward we went for pizza? Do you remember when Mason's bike broke, and you fixed it? Remember that day you were babysitting, and there was a Tornado Warning. And we hid in the basement with a huge tub of ice cream?"

Jason's eyes twitched. His mouth flickered.

"I'm willing to give Dad so many chances, and I know that makes you mad, but if something happens to you, Jason, I won't be okay. I love Dad. But I *need* you."

Jason's head finally tilted toward Grayson. Grayson concentrated harder to keep the flames away, to shelter himself with a dome of arctic air.

"Look at me, Jace." Tears froze to Grayson's cheeks. He let his armor melt away, just enough to show his face to his brother. "Please. Stay with us."

Jason's scowl melted into horrified confusion.

"Mason and I both need you," Grayson continued. "We need our brother to watch out for us, to figure out problems with us, to teach us stuff. Because maybe Dad won't always be there. Someday Mom and Dad will both be gone. And all we'll have is each other."

"Silence!" the Grand Sulfurian's voice exploded like thunder.

"Jason, this rage, it's not your fault. They did this to you." He pointed up at the Grand Sulfurian with his Frost-Blade. "But I know you can control it. You're better than that monster up there. You're my hero, Jason. You always were. And I need you to help me save this city."

Jason's face finally melted into total recognition.

The aura of fire dimmed.

"Gray..." Jason reached out, but yellow fire sparked between them. "I think it's too late, Gray. Get out of here. I don't know how this happened, but... I can't stop it."

"No! That's what that sun-dried doofus wants you to think!" Grayson pushed forward. He used his Frost-Blade to smother the fire surrounding his brother. "We can fix this together. But I need you to just... be cool. Let me help."

"Be cool?" Jason panicked. "Gray, I feel like my head is about to explode into a volcano. I don't want you here! You're not safe!"

"Grayson," Mason's voice came in. "How close are you?"

"Almost there, Mace." Grayson pushed back the inferno of heat. "Listen, Jason, calm down as much as you can, and trust us. Mason is going to talk me through this, and we're going to save you."

"There is no stopping it, Frost-Keeper," The Grand Sulfurian shouted above them. "The flames of the Sulfurian Empire are eternal!"

"Grayson, go!" Jason cried. "Any second now, that monster is going to win. I can't hold it back any longer."

Grayson managed to push the last of the fire away. He grabbed his brother's shoulder with an icy hand. But Jason's eyes glowed brighter. Hotter. "Mason. I'm as close as I'm going to get."

"Take the Frost-Key, and hold it up to one of Jason's eyes." Mason instructed.

"I don't like where this is going," Grayson pulled his Frost-Blade back into the handle of his key. He held the key to the inferno of his brother's right eye.

"Trust me," Mason instructed. "Just close your

eyes. Picture the germ. It's lodged in Jason's sinus."

Grayson panicked. "What's the sinus?"

"It's a cavity, behind the eyes, between your nose and brain. Think of Victor's diagram."

Grayson closed his eyes. He remembered the picture from the book.

"There's already water in Jason's body. In everyone's body," Mason explained. "You don't have to stab through his head or cut into him to kill the germ. You just have to tap into that water on a molecular level."

"Okay." Grayson inhaled deeply. If he could manipulate river water, fire hydrants, and fire hoses, he could do this too.

"It's a quick freeze of the bare minimum amount of tissue around the germ," Mason explained. "If you do it right, Jason will be fine. But if you overdo it..."

"I understand." Grayson concentrated. *Victor, all you other Frost-Keepers,* he thought. *Help me out here.*

"You cannot stop it, Frost Keeper," The Grand Sulfurian bellowed. "You will kill him! And I will still rise in the husk of his corpse."

Grayson's hand trembled.

Suddenly, he felt a firm grip on his shoulder. "Gray," Jason said. "You got this. I trust you, brother."

Grayson pictured the germ, squeezed the handle of the key, and sent a micro-pulse of cold into his brother's head.

Jason screamed in agony. He collapsed forward into Grayson's arms and fell to his knees. For one horrible moment, Grayson was sure that he had failed.

But then Jason's hands reached up and massaged

his temples. "Ow!" he shouted. "That is the worst ice cream headache I have ever had in my life!"

All the heat and fire swirled away from Jason. The yellow aura dissipated.

The Grand Sulfurian's bearded face spread into a massive "O" of surprise. His white-hot eyes faded. The glowing portal rippled away like molten lava, revealing cloudy, gray sky above. The cold dark of night returned, and the entire city fell dead quiet.

Grayson glanced around. The fire was gone. The lights of the Chicago Skyline were lit up. Crowds of civilians started cheering from the streets below. Fire engines sounded their horns. Police Sirens wailed in victory.

Grayson helped his brother to his feet. "Jason, you all right?" He melted his ice armor away.

Jason pulled his brother into a huge hug. His voice broke, "You are the craziest, most awesome brother!"

Grayson squeezed him back. "I'm sorry. I didn't know you were in danger until it was too late."

Jason pulled back. "No, I'm sorry. I've been a jerk to you, all day. All summer. Gray, I love you, you and Mason both. I'm always going to be here for you. No matter what. You know that, right?"

Grayson smiled. "I know." He gazed up at the clouds, then back out at the scores of lights over the city. "It's been a long, hot day, Jace. What do you say we give these people a cool reward?"

Grayson stepped away from his brother. He sprouted his Frost-Blade and aimed it at the clouds.

A beam of icy-white shot into the sky, and moments later, tufts of fluffy white snow drifted over the City of Chicago in peak July.

Chapter 36

One week later, life in Chicago was mostly back to normal—except of course for the Slynt Hotel being shut down for a thorough inspection. Once all the danger had subsided, however, Lucy's dad couldn't have been more thrilled about the development.

"You can't buy this kind of publicity!" he had raved to Grayson and Lucy the morning after the Sulfurians' defeat. "The whole world saw a superhero thwart an evil invasion on a Slynt property, and *nobody* got hurt!"

Grayson wanted to clarify that the Sulfurians did hurt people, and that there could still be more of them out there, but he didn't want to cause trouble. As much as he trusted Lucy, he still wasn't convinced that Alexander Slynt was the best confidant for the Frost-Keeper.

Even so, Slynt had given Mason and Lucy an unlimited budget to adapt the Water Tower into a 21st century headquarters. They were soon equipped with flat screen monitors, cutting edge computer systems, and high-tech gadgets so complex, Grayson was actually worried his brother wouldn't have any idea how to use them.

But Mason was catching on fast.

Jason helped with the remodeling, since the restaurant and ice cream shop remained closed along with the Slynt. The three brothers spent their evenings exploring Victor Drake's journal. There was so much Grayson still didn't understand about his job as the Frost-Keeper, but in a short time, he learned that his predecessors had clashed swords with more than just Sulfurians.

It took some convincing from all three brothers, but Aunt Linda agreed to keep Gray's new job on the downlow from their parents, at least until the end of the summer. There was a lot going on in all of their lives, and more than anything, Grayson didn't want his parents to worry.

The Frost-Keeper made very few appearances in the days following the Sulfurian invasion. Grayson was trying to decide how to use his powers, when to use them, and why.

One night, after his brothers had gone home, Gray found a passage in Victor Drake's book.

It is important that the Frost-Keeper maintain an active role in his community and his world. But it is not the Frost-Keeper's job to police humanity and protect them from themselves. It has always been my burden to know where that line should be drawn.

Grayson thought about the prospects of using his powers to stop criminals and extinguish fires, both natural and manmade. He had incredible power, but he couldn't be everywhere at once.

He couldn't help everyone all the time from every threat.

And he still had so much to learn.

One night, he sat on a bench outside the Water

Tower and watched tourists and Chicagoans hurry by. Street musicians played on the corner. The sky glowed soft orange as the sun set beyond the skyline.

"May I sit?" Lucy Slynt's emerald eyes shimmered. Her blond locks curled over her shoulders.

"*Mais, bien sur!*" Grayson said.

"*Mon Dieu!*" Lucy sat. "*Parlez-vous Francaise?*"

"Not really," Grayson admitted. "But Jason taught me a few phrases."

"*Très bien.*" Lucy bit her lip. She rested her hand on the bench. Her fingers twitched.

Grayson reached over and took her hand in his. "Not too cold for you, is it?"

"No," she said. "You're very warm... at the moment, at least."

"Cool." Grayson squeezed her palm. "I've been thinking a lot about all these people coming and going."

"What about them?"

"Well, there are so many of them. So many people in the world." Grayson felt the handle of the Frost-Key in his other pocket. "I'm still wondering: Why me?"

Lucy kissed his cheek. "I don't wonder at all."

About the Author

Kevin M. Folliard is a writer of books for young readers, including *Violet Black & the Curse of Camp Coldwater*, *Jake Carter & the Nightmare Gallery*, *Jimmy Chimaera & the Temple of Champions*, and *Matt Palmer & the Komodo Uprising*. His adult fiction has been collected by The Horror Tree, Flame Tree Publishing, The Dread Machine, and more. His recent publications include his novella "Tower of Raven" from Demain Publishing and his 2020 horror anthology *The Misery King's Closet*. Kevin currently resides in the Chicagoland area, where he enjoys his day job as an academic writing advisor and membership in the La Grange and Brookfield Writers Groups. When not writing or working, he's usually reading Stephen King, playing Tetris, or traveling the U.S.A.

Orphans in Londinium never have easy lives,
but they're especially brutal in the ashfall.
Patty Rinkin, a factory grindery girl with a rare last name,
just wants to survive.
But when she finds a dragon's egg among the filth,
things might just change.
Can Patty fight back against the Gear to end the people's suffering?

Dragons
OF THE
Ashfall

BOOK ONE OF THE
WAR OF LEAVES AND SCALES
BY

Jonathon Mast

A STEAMPUNK FANTASY ADVENTURE
FOR YOUNG READERS
THAT YOU WON'T FORGET!

 Available in paperback and on Kindle
www.darkowlpublishing.com

COME TO DARK OWL'S WEBSITE
AND VISIT

The
Young Readers
Bookstore

OUR CURRENT AND UPCOMING YOUNG
READER BOOKS ARE FOR A VARIETY OF
READING LEVELS!

**And we rate the appropriateness of all
Dark Owl's books on our YR Bookstore page.**

Visit us at
www.darkowlpublishing.com/the-yr-bookstore

And we're on